Woman Of My Dreams

Woman Of My Dreams

PAUL HANLIN, JR.

To my mom and dad,
the best parents a son could hope to have,
and to Eliza Dushku,
my #1 choice to play Gillian in the movie version.

Chapter 1

William Ross' day was just getting better and better.

He had taken her out to dinner for a second time, and now they were at his apartment. She was dark-haired, perfect olive skin, a blue DKNY dress, and a voice that could induce smoke inhalation it was so sexy.

"Thanks for a terrific time tonight," she said, cradling his hands together. "But according to my watch, there's a lot of night left."

"Yeah," Ross said; he's been in this spot before, but few times compared to this. "Do you want to come in for a nightcap? I don't normally do this on a second date, but . . . good Lord, you are so beautiful. You sure you don't have a boyfriend?"

"Why do you ask?" she wondered.

"Because someone like you usually is spoken for by the time I get around to finding her. I'm glad I was early for a change," Ross stated, gingerly embracing her waist.

She smiled, her rose red lips glistening. "You've been most respectful, and I appreciate that. You're a guy I can trust. So let's do this." Next moment, she kissed him square on the lips, again and again. "I'm yours, Will. Completely yours. Together there's nothing we can't accomplish." She opens the door that he unlocked and they're kissing like there's no tomorrow. Ross cannot contain himself; he's never felt this much passion toward any woman in his entire time on earth. They tumble onto his bed in the two-room apartment.

Ross leaps up from his bed, in the dead of night; the clock to his right says 3:45 AM, and there is no one around. He is drenched in sweat, even though it's fall. That couldn't have been a dream, he swore to himself; it was real. As vivid and true to life as life can get.

Yet it was nothing but a dream that reverberated through every part of his body on a late Sunday night, which would beget Monday morning. That most assuredly sucked; he had a couple extra vacation days he took after the event that really went south on him, which wounded his very soul. Still, a dream like that almost made up for it. He would be back in work in about 5 hours, back among his friends, his co-workers, doing what he does best.

Ross took some consolation as he struggled to doze back off; maybe she could drop by his dream world again; the sooner the better. It certainly ended on a high note.

Chapter 2

The alarm woke him up at exactly 7 AM, Ross feeling every bit of his 41 years as he rolled out of bed and made breakfast. William decided that he had had enough of spending time in his apartment and that it was as good a moment as any to get back to work. After all, he was the editor of San Diego's most successful weekly newspaper and maybe that comfort would take his mind off of the recent past.

He left his third floor studio apartment at the Treo Condominium on Kettner Boulevard and "A" Street in the heart of downtown, a half-mile from Little Italy, a couple blocks from the city's own version of Broadway at 8:30 AM for the 15-minute walk to the 900 block of "E" Street. Ross's mind kept flashing back to the dream he had earlier; dreams are just that, only dreams, but every detail about this one was as real as the buildings and people he was passing—a world which had been far more blissful and good to him than the real world had been of late.

The key would be to just keep going as if nothing had happened. Put it in the rear-view mirror and move on. The quicker he did that, he could recover that much faster. Ross was a little over six feet tall, dark brown hair, with a touch of gray here and there, hazel eyes, and a somewhat stocky build, but nothing like a year ago, when he was given a choice; to lose weight, or in the bluntest terms possible, die. He chose the former, and not only cut his body mass index by almost 25%, but his total weight by a third. It changed his life after years of letting himself go by eating anything and everything in sight, it seemed. Those demons would stay with him for the rest of his days, he figured, but like an alcoholic battling an addiction, it would be one day at a time. The knowledge that he had the mother of all dream dates, literally speaking, would also be first aid that he welcomed in that particular daily battle.

William's commute was uneventful, fortunately, as the Library Lofts beckoned from a few blocks away. His friends were witness to his agony, and he would have to deal with it, with them around him. That, however, was not on his list of priorities at the moment. One day, maybe; just not now.

Not when the wounds were fresh—and still most raw.

The third-floor offices of CityLife, San Diego's newest, cutting-edge and vastly popular weekly newspaper, is bustling with activity on this sunny Monday. Most of the writers are in work already, putting the finishing touches on the following week's stories.

Ross's inner circle includes Dan McCall, the chief sportswriter, 33 years old; Brian Vincent, the lifestyles scribe; African-American and 32; Rebecca Holm, who turned 35 the week before; brown-haired blue-eyed, and the fashion correspondent; Amy Lloyd, also 35 and married with one child; she's their entertainment writer, and 42 year old Barry Greene, the assistant editor, the one who answers to Ross himself.

"Hey, all; it's been quite the week, hasn't it, folks?" ruefully suggested Greene, medium build, dark hair, brown eyes as he took his seat.

"It's especially comforting that sometimes when life sucks, it can suck even worse," McCall replied, keeping up the tone of irony that permeated the conversation. "Nobody saw it coming; that's the worst part."

"Not even Will," Greene joined in. "He had a glazed look about him, like it didn't register for a minute or two . . . and then asking us to join him at Mickey D's for a quick dinner. I'm worried about him."

Holm took the point. "He's been out for a couple of days; there's no telling when he'll be back; at any rate, we've got to give him a lot of latitude when he does."

"And longitude, and whatever else," Vincent finished the thought. "Whenever he does return, let's be there for him—"

"You're already here now, Brian." A familiar face greeted them with a semi-smile. "Good morning, everybody."

"William!" Holm yelled, stunned that he was there. The quintet got up from their desks and welcomed him back. "We thought you'd want to take a few more days off."

"What 'Becca said," Vincent continued. "You OK?"

"I'm surviving," Ross assured them. "Down time can be a double-edged sword; it can heal wounds, but too much of it can drive you batty. It makes you think too much about the bad shit and can draw you away from the things, and the people that matter. I've had my mourning, and it's time to get in the game again."

The group was taken aback by his confession. "It's just that you weren't exactly yourself last week; who would be after something like that?" McCall told him. "We're all here for you if you want to vent; God knows you have a right to."

"Thanks for the offer, but I do think we have a staff meeting in the conference room. At some point, yeah. Just not now, not when the memories are fresh, OK?" Ross asked his colleagues, who nodded in approval. "So; what's on the agenda for today?"

Ross was back; to business as usual, after a week where unusual happenings were an understatement.

Chapter 3

William drove from work to a place called Nighttime, a dance club near the Mission District. It was one of the newer, fast-rising in popularity places for folks to unwind and meet/greet. It was where he would go after a particularly rough day. This day wasn't that rough, but he felt like going there anyway, to get his mind off what had happened before he went on his unscheduled leave of absence. The club was semi-packed, which meant folks could actually dance without bumping into other couples while doing it.

Ross was at the bar sipping an orange juice; Darling Violetta's "Cure" was playing on the turntable when someone cozied up to him.

"Hey, handsome; back for more, huh?"

He couldn't believe it; it was the woman from his dream, in the chair to his left.

"Goodness; I don't even know your name or your phone number and now I've met you twice in two nights. This is beyond good luck."

"I liked what I saw—and heard," she said, motioning him to the center of the club. "Wanna dance?"

Both William and his date grooved to the music, but that didn't stop him from trying to find out more about his companion. "I was wondering if I'm going to see you again. I didn't have the chance to ask you last time—"

"I'll be here as long as you want me to be. You're saying and doing all the right things, William. I like you a lot. You're the first guy I've been involved with; ever."

"You're shittin' me. I am?" Ross was beyond surprised. She was so good-looking, so sexy, and so confident in herself without being overbearing. All the qualities he had hoped for in a woman, and they were all on display here and now.

"The first—and maybe only one." She kissed him impulsively full on the lips, holding nothing back; her sweet perfume was not that overpowering, but just right, and it drove his insides to distraction. "Eminently kissable, too." Her voice was as fetching as her body; raspy to the point of melting any defenses he may have put up. "My place this time?"

She caught him off-guard with that one. "Your place? Whatever might you be suggesting?" he said in mock seriousness.

"A nightcap which tops what we're doing here and now. If you want to take the chance, that is." The moment was right; it was true; it wasn't a snow job. Fate had brought them together, William knew. It wasn't the first time he would go down this road, but it would be, he suspected, a joyride with the emphasis on joy . . .

And then he woke up. Again.

He was in his bed, his apartment, alone. At least he had slept a bit later than the prior night. It was 5:30 AM. Another startlingly vivid dream had salved his soul. He thought he would be mad that the dream ended just as it was about to get good. Ross wasn't, however, in the slightest.

Maybe sleep would be something to look forward to instead of dreading. He had thoughts of his own mortality as he tried to doze off, especially in the past couple of years. Now it seemed like he had a friend who could join him in his down time. Even better, someone who he could keep to himself and not tell a living soul about.

After the month he's had, Ross figured the fates owed him at least some bliss. He looked forward to the day's workload, and more so to the night, which would follow in short order.

Chapter 4

William brought a newfound energy to his work during the day, which was matched (and surpassed on occasion over the next two weeks) by his nights, where his dream world was one very active place.

He wined her, dined her, and loved her with unbridled abandon. Slowly, the emotional carnage he went through had subsided greatly. And it was his secret alone. No one else needed to know; at any rate, who would believe him? The dreams had become even more realistic, if that was even possible. As great as it was, he was getting a bit drained by them, and he suggested to his co-workers that they have a get-together at a restaurant on a Friday.

Thursday night, however, Ross had trouble falling asleep. A particularly boisterous lightning storm which swept over the city during the overnight hours had kept him up for a few hours. When he finally dozed off, his female companion was nowhere to be found in his slumber.

As Friday beckoned, Ross came to the realization that this was a sign from up above to get back to living again, in the actual, real world. I've had three terrific weeks, with the pain that he felt being washed away. Like the title of the final episode of Star Trek: The Next Generation so aptly put it,

All good things . . .

Friday came, and the dinner was set at Jimmy Love's restaurant in the Gaslamp Quarter; it took up two floors in the Old City Hall building, and it was well on its way to being packed, even with the resumption of the foul weather of the night before.

"We haven't had many occasions to shoot the breeze of late," suggested Holm, "So I figured today would be a good time to chill."

"Especially with the electrical storm we're having right now . . . sheez," marveled Vincent. "You don't have many of those happening out here. Even all the weather folks got caught off-guard."

"On top of that, did anyone catch that meteor shower last night before the lightning came?" Greene wondered aloud. "Clear as a bell last night, it was just awesome seeing those things zip across the sky. Got some great footage with the camcorder."

"Timing is everything," Ross said, pulling out four small envelopes from his pocket. "I had a meeting with the parent company of ours, and we've had an exceptional quarter, circulation and finance-wise, so now's as good a time as any to give you all these," he handed them out to his friends.

"At least they're not pink-colored; that's something," quipped Lloyd. "It's not December, so it's not bonuses, obviously."

Ross smiled as they opened them, and the mood changed to an even better mode. "Rate of inflation only, but it's still something. You yourselves made this possible." He raised his glass of orange juice for them to follow suit. "A toast to the best group of writers I've had the privilege of working for. Your hard work and dedication have made CityLife one of the best weeklies on the left coast—even if the Padres don't care for Dan's op-ed pieces on what needs to be fixed."

McCall smiled at that. He had rankled the feathers of the inhabitants of Qualcomm Stadium more than once during the Padres' downward spiral.

"So how's Cindy, Dan?"

"New job interview with the Union-Trib in the next week or so. We're good. Are you?"

"Am I . . ." Ross was a bit confused.

"You holding up OK? It's been a couple weeks; you seem to be getting back to normal," Vincent offered a tentative appraisal of his boss' mood.

"I have been mending, thanks. Time does heal a lot of stuff, and the more time you put between yourself and the wreckage that you were at ground zero of, the less it hurts. I've been dealing with it. Maybe I won't even have to burden you with my moaning after all."

"Now, Will," Lloyd interjected quickly, "We're a group; you believed in us when few would and the least we can do is to return the favor when one of our own got tossed in the sausage grinder."

"What Amy said," Rebecca added. "Things weren't exactly life-is-a-cabaret-esque of late for you. You got the smack down laid on you, and we want you to know that we're there—"

"I do appreciate the kind words. People deal with bad stuff in their own way. I know the drill; denial is not just a river. I'm just not ready yet to dump my problems on you all yet. At some point, yes; but I guess even three weeks later isn't quite enough time to—"

That laugh. That voice.

She's here. Right here in this restaurant, and it was no damned dream this time. "Would you excuse me for a moment?"

Ross got up and looked around the entire place for her; but she was nowhere to be found. She was here, dammit; somehow.

Or maybe his mind had finally snapped after all. He walked back to the table where they were, now in a state of confusion; he couldn't dare tell them the truth; they'd know he went round the bend.

"What's going on?" asked a sympathetic Greene. "You all right, Will?"

"Yeah. I thought I heard somebody from my days back East. False alarm." The time had come to face reality, however reluctantly he felt. "The weekend's coming up; it's going to rain Monday. Can't think of a better time to come clean; although you may all wind up with ears so bent you'll lose half your hearing."

"No prob, Will," McCall nodded and spoke for a grateful group. "We'll deal with it then."

Ross sighed a whopper of relief, and his co-workers felt the same. At least he'd have one more weekend of bliss before he returned to the real world.

Chapter 5

Saturday morning. Sunny skies abounded, and time to go to the laundromat a few blocks away from his apartment for his weekly wash and dry. The place is empty for the moment, but that always changes. He opens the door and proceeds to put his laundry into one of the industrial-strength machines. He's got time to kill, so he brought some reading material with him. He discovers, however, something else is in the place with him.

A cat. Must've darted in while the door was closing, and now he was purring and stationary just a few feet away. Ross always liked cats, even though he could never keep one around due to being allergic to them for any length of time. So he thought of something to keep his sanity intact, especially after last night's events.

"Well, at least I'll have some company here." He motioned for the cat to come over, which it did, to his surprise. "Tell you what; I've had quite the past half-month . . . I don't know if folk like you dream, but I've been front and center in late nights any guy would kill to be in my place. They say there aren't angels in human form who walk this earth. I'm one who would like to offer a rebuttal to that.

"Picture a feline cat; OK, redundant, there—who's everything you've envisioned; everything you've hoped for on the inside as well as out. Now see her right smack in front of you, in all her off-the-charts beauty. Further, she has the hots for you, too, and you make a connection. Pretty soon afterward, she's all you think about, every waking—and non-waking—moment. The only thing that keeps you going on your way back from hell." The cat didn't move a muscle, but the one talking to it was clearly not there; he was somewhere else. Back in the past, where it had dealt him a rotten hand. Ross was on the brink of tears, but quickly composed himself. "Yeah, I'm going all Deborah Gibson on ya, as she's only in my dreams. Tell you what, though; I've never felt more wanted, happier or sated when she visits me when the covers get pulled up—"

"Dude, Debbie Gibson? The musician Tiffany longed to be but wasn't?"

Another voice. Ross' blood turned ice-cold. His entire body was goose bump city. It was behind him, so he got up and turned around . . .

What he saw first were her legs, bronzed to perfection. He saw the white miniskirt next, followed by her black top, contrasted with stunning detail. The jet-black hair, lustrous and long, which draped down to her firm and shapely chest. Then the eyes. Looking right at him, smiling sweetly.

"This sure beats seeing you only at night. I'm flattered that I have that much of an effect on you."

Ross' knees buckled from under him. Standing not a yard away from him was the woman he's kept company with only at night, and far from the realm of reality. He collapses an instant later.

"William!" she rushed over to him, who landed on his backside. He seemed OK, but the woman grabbed a chair and helped him onto it. It took a few moments for the cobwebs to get out of Dodge, but clear they did. She smiled as she squatted down to be at eye-level with him.

"That's quite a unique way to say hello," she said mischievously.

Ross couldn't believe his eyes, ears, or other three senses. "Am I dreaming again? No, not this time; not this time, goddammit," he got up and paced around the still-empty laundromat. "I had dinner with my co-workers last night. I woke up from a sound sleep, and this is Saturday, and that's laundry day. But you're here, which officially makes this THE most lifelike dream I've had ever."

"Hate to burst your bubble, my friend, but this is no dream. 'Not this time' is right. Think of it as a crossing over John Edward would shit in his pants to have on his show." She sees the dryers and can look at herself in the reflection of one of the clear glass casings. "I must say, you did an absolute kick-ass job. Your powers of creation are exceptional."

"But . . ." his voice trailed off, mesmerized; transfixed by what was before him.

"C'mon, Will, you weren't so dumbstruck and tongue-tied when we first met. I guess I can make allowances, though. To see the look on your face right now . . ." she smiled a whopper, her blinding white teeth contrasting spectacularly with her red lips.

"What are—I mean, *who* are you?"

"My name is Gillian, and for the past month, give or take, I've had the pleasure—an understatement of profound proportion—to make your acquaintance," she said, walking toward him slowly, confidently. "We've talked, we've danced; we've loved—especially that—and you have been the utmost gentleman every step of the way." She offered her right hand to him.

Which he took and shook it. "Gillian; in the time I've been with you in these dreams, I don't recall ever asking you your name."

"You're an X-Files fan. You had a major crush on Scully. You liked the way 'Gillian' sounded," she didn't want to scare him away so she kept her distance for the moment. "I know you've probably got a list of questions stretching from one end of the country to the other. I'll do my best to answer all of 'em," she promised.

"Yeah; I'm not usually reduced to one-word answers by choice, but . . ." Ross marveled at how utterly beautiful Gillian was. "May I?"

He impulsively walked toward her and embraced her in his arms, wanting to hold onto every last moment of his best morning in a long, long time. "If this is perchance a dream, God, thanks for sending an angel my way."

Gillian smiled and separated from him ever so slightly. "May I?" She motioned down to where his hands were. Ross nodded as she took his left hand, raised it up with her right. "You're right; this is only a dream, like you said." She guided his hand toward herself, and made his hand gently press against her left breast.

Ross fidgeted noticeably, but Gillian's piercing eyes withered away any self-doubt he had, or the will to pull his hand away from her. She then kissed him right on the money for almost 30 seconds non-stop.

"Still think this is just a dream, William?" she said playfully as he held her close and planted a kiss of his own on her achingly awesome lips. "I don't know about you, but I'm starving for another thing right now. Anyplace where we can get some breakfast?"

"I believe that can be arranged." Ross said without hesitation. He still had a mountain of time before he had to worry about putting his stuff in the dryer. Even if that weren't the case, he'd *make* the time. By any means necessary. Fate had given him a much-needed shot in the arm, and he wasn't about to waste the opportunity. He held out his right arm at the elbow. "Shall we?"

She accepted, and they walked out of the laundromat to his car. To the most memorable morning meal he would ever have. To a new chapter in his life, one filled with joy, not pain or sameness.

Chapter 6

It was a little after 9 when William and Gillian had their breakfast date at a small restaurant about a half-mile from the laundromat. Gillian's eyes took everything in; the smell of the eggs and coffee, the other customers in the place; but mostly, her mentor, and how he conducted himself. A waitress came over to their table.

"Hi, folks; what would you like to have today?"

"I'll go for your killer good American cheese omelet, side order of home fries, and coffee, decaf."

"One down, one to go. What will you have?"

The one thing Gillian didn't do while she was soaking everything in was to look at the menu. She looked at Ross with a hint of trepidation, and then said, "I'll have what he's having."

"Two it is, then. Won't be long." She leaves them alone. Ross notices her tentativeness.

"I forgot to think—every single thing, no matter how mundane for any of us, will be a completely new experience for you. It can be overwhelming, but you can rest assured I'll be there for you."

"Thanks, Will." Her mood was more relaxed, now that she knew he was looking out for her.

"Gillian, I'm sorry I said 'what are you?' before I corrected myself. It was inconsiderate of me; like you were a thing instead of—"

"Inconsiderate? Hardly. I would've asked the same thing. What am I? It's a fair question. I come from a place where potential is limitless, where there is no 'can't', where all things are possible. Your mind."

"My mind?"

"Every living soul on this earth has a mental picture of a companion, an ideal friend, a fantasy. What I am, who I am and what I look like, sprung from your mind's eye. The dreams you had of us together was the rocket fuel, and the crazy stuff that went on last week was the ignition."

"The electrical storm . . . we also had a meteor shower last week. That doesn't explain how you showed up in the laundromat. No one had come in the door, since I was facing it."

"The place was empty, and I decided there was no time like the present. I didn't want to interrupt your soliloquy; you let your guard down a bit. You showed your true feeling toward me, and I'm grateful. I'm only one part of your essence, Will. You, ultimately, were the catalyst in bringing me from your mind into your world."

"Great; I'm Andrew McCarthy and you're Kim Cattrall," Ross quipped as their breakfasts were served. Both refrained from saying anything else until the waitress left.

"I'm so that much prettier than Kimmy." Gillian cautiously took her first bite from the sweet-looking omelet, Ross watching to see how she would react. Her eyes were the first clue he sought; an emerging smile, bright as sun glare on a driver. "Wow!"

"Wow is right; you're certainly not one at a loss for confidence."

"Just like you. I know you, Will, since I came from your very thoughts. You want a woman to be strong, to be sure of herself, to be . . . well-endowed," she stated with a wink of her eye, and Ross's face turned a dozen different shades of red. "You want, more than anything else, a woman of substance. All the qualities you want in a lady, I possess them. I know what thrills you and what scares you— for the most part, anyway, and I'm here because you asked for me."

"I don't understand; how did I 'ask' for you?"

She took his hands in her own and leaned over slightly toward him. "For all your success, there's been utter sadness. Something affected you that deeply, that painfully, that you turned to the one thing that could sustain you through it; me."

Ross was a bit unnerved now; how could she have known about what happened? Maybe she didn't, or else she would have said it already. He wasn't prepared to share that event with her—not yet, not on her first day of her life away from the darkness of his dreams.

"All the qualities I'm looking for in a woman, you said, right? What about that?" William pointed to her right wrist, where something ringed it, and it wasn't a watch.

"You noticed; the tattoo was my idea. I've tried to tell you what I am; now the time's at hand to tell you what I'm *not*. I'm not an alien, or an anti-Christ, or an evil force seeking global domination. I'm here because you've proven in our time spent that you are a man worth getting to know, and I want to, for however long we have together, be with you. To experience your world, to see the people who have shaped you and work with you.

"I know this is an awful lot to absorb, Will, but the honesty that you were born with precludes me from lying about any of this. I do owe my very existence to you; when you get down to cases, you created me in your own image-"

"Oh, I don't know if I want to go there; I mean I'm no God. Far, farther and farthest from that."

"You're enough of one in my book," Gillian replied without the slightest hesitation. "That said, don't expect me to be bossed around too much, or have me saying shit about being your humble servant or any of that; my admiration of you does go only so far." She tried to put up a stern front in saying this, but it kind of failed miserably.

Ross' mouth was agape with wonder. She was every bit his equal, she could sling the one-liner with the best of his friends. Gillian was an intimidating presence—and he loved it. "Jesus, you're good; there is one thing, though, that we do need to work on this weekend."

"Ah . . . wanting to find out if our extracurricular activities are just as fantastic on this side of the aisle? How typical," Gillian tossed him a wicked smile.

"No, not that; not yet, anyway," Ross countered, finishing up his meal. "It's your wardrobe; I don't think you have one, just what you have on."

"Yeah, now that you say it. Serves me right for jumping to conclusions." She did likewise with her food. "That was spectacular; don't mind me if you hear that a lot this weekend. Everything is so new to me, so virgin. What did you have in mind?"

Chapter 7

The Fashion Valley Mall was in their midst. San Diego's premier shopping marketplace would be their home away from home for, as it turned out, the next six hours. They hit all the major women's stores; Ann Taylor, Lane Bryant, the Limited—and Victoria's Secret, all on Ross' dime. He built up quite the nest egg due to his parents constantly drumming in him the value of putting money in the bank. When it was all said and done, he put out almost $1,850 in suits, tops, dresses, shoes, etc. for his companion—and whatever she tried on she looked spectacular. After everything was loaded in the trunk, William said just three words to Gillian:

"Let's go home."

Her heart soared. He trusted her enough to bring her into his most personal place; his apartment. Not before they ordered pizzas, though; this would be a night to eat in for a change.

At the front door of his apartment, adjacent to Balboa Park at Olive Avenue and 6th Street, William had the two pizzas in hand, while Gillian had two bags filled to overflowing with clothes, and another two sitting there.

"A pretty nice occasion, this," he said as he got out his room key. "I'd like to officially invite you into my home, Gillian. For as long as you want to stay."

"Will, you've done so much for me; you've eased my transition into your life. You're a good man. I knew that all along, though, and to see what lengths you've gone to ease my fears prove to me that you're the shit."

"Thanks; I think," Ross smiled; she can talk a blue streak and still look and sound completely real in doing so. He opened the door to his apartment. "Lady first."

She emerged into his apartment and just stood there, taking it all in. The apartment was about 700 square feet; it had a kitchenette and a medium-sized dining table, and was sprinkled with a sofa and two additional couches. To the left was a home entertainment center with a TV, VCR and Xbox video game system with a stack of sports games; to the right was a home computer, his trusty AMD Athlon 1.1 GHz system, a full one-third slower than the ever-changing standard of fastness, but it still served him most well. High ceilings, and blue-painted walls. Further back were the bathroom and his modest bedroom. She walked around, looking at every nook and cranny, impressed by its depth and size. Gillian went into the bedroom, the place where they both spent a lot of time together even before she became flesh and blood. Ross followed her in where he was met by a sultry, jaw-dropping kiss from his no-longer-a-dream lover.

"This is a dope apartment, Will; I'm impressed."

"Dope?" he feigned shock at that. "No such substance here; in fact, no drink, no smoke, no drugs for me—the new three-strikes rule, as in if a girl finds out he doesn't do any of 'em, he's history. You want that kind of guy in your life?"

"It's a woman's loss if she thinks that way." She turned toward him, and helped herself to the pizza box, putting it on the dining table. "Let's eat, yo?"

So Will and Gillian are eating their pizza as Dido's "Here with Me" is playing on the radio. As he finished his first slice, he took off his shoes and socks. When Gillian finished hers, she took off her shoes as well. Which inspired her companion to a unique idea.

When he finished his second slice, Ross took off his designer T-shirt. Gillian looked at him quizzically, and then the recognition struck her. She finished her slice, took off her belt and unbuttoned her blouse. A silent game of 'strip pizza' was underway, with each consumed slice meaning another piece of clothing came off until they were in their skivvies.

Which they shed when they went into his bedroom, where Gillian and William made breathtaking, mind-numbing love all night long, each showing endurance to the other as if there was no tomorrow. Ross didn't know he had this much stamina, such drive. It was safe to think she was equally driven and that her passion was seemingly bottomless.

It was 4:30 AM by the time they came up for air. They were sprawled on his king-size bed, exhausted, elated. It fell on Ross to comment on the catalyst to their night of off-the-meter wildness.

"I know one thing; I'll never look at pizza the same way again." Both erupted into laughter. "I love you, Gillian. You've been my salvation, my rock."

"Love you more. You're pretty darn good, Will."

"Time for me to say 'wow' for a change," he said ruefully. I've had girlfriends and relationships in my life, but you didn't raise the bar—you torched it."

"I believe the phrase you're looking for is 'mad skills'," Gillian's round, firm body rolled over to be next to him, both under his covers, both stark naked. "I love this world. It has so much potential, so much possibility and promise, but one thing makes it truly worth living for—this world has you. Thank you for the shopping spree today. Just the right mix of proper, down-to-earth . . . and borderline naughty."

"Yeah, there was an ulterior motive to get you in the Secret store, I must admit that. I'm glad you were a good sport about it."

"Girl's gotta have some fun," she joked. "I will overlook your unfortunate foray into sexist-ness."

"Hey now," Ross protested, albeit meekly, since he was guilty as charged. "Shit, you got me. Imagine that—an actual night of whoopee and not a candle in sight."

"Yeah; it's all romantic and stuff, but what if either of 'em get a bit rough and knock one of the candles over? Body parts wouldn't be the only things that would be up. As in up in smoke." he smiled. "We've a few more hours before dawn."

"What do you want to do today?"

"Leave the credit card at home and spend Sunday showing

you San Diego. The grand tour; there's a lot for you to see, and I'd be honored if I could be your guide," Ross said with utter sincerity. He knew he had something special here and would not screw around with the karma gods that would mess it up.

"William Ross; I accept your generous invite. I thought I knew you enough from being with you in my world. But I was wrong. It's even better." Both of them kissed again and again and reveled in each other's company some more.

Chapter 8

They toured San Diego at their own leisure, hitting all the sights, basking in yet another cloudless sunny day, and strengthening their exploding relationship. As the day progresses, Ross realized that he had a tough decision to make. He would have to go to work the following day, and that would mean leaving Gillian to her own devices. More so, how would he handle it with his co-workers? Would he at all? And how would she react to whatever way he went?

They eventually returned around 8PM, had dinner and retired for the night. William had a surprise for Gillian as she was about to get into bed. It was a newspaper.

"Not just any newspaper, I presume," she knew enough to deduce this was something special to him. "CityLife; this is your paper, isn't it?" Gillian's face lit up with recognition.

"Editor in chief. That's what allowed me to be financially semi-secure for the moment. I came out here 6 years ago. I was a journalist who wanted more to run a newspaper, not just be a part of one. So I had some experience back in Philly as an associate editor for a bi-weekly newspaper and when CityLife's editor position was open, I figured I'd take a shot at it. I had writing and editing experience; the paper's parent company took a chance on me and I got an assistant editor job four years ago. When the editor decided to move on due to wanting to be closer to his family up north, I got the call. I let some people go, hired others and we found the right chemistry. I wasn't a boss to them, nor are, but more of a friend. We've gotten along great, and that translates into the product we put out. We have a circulation of over 175,000 in San Diego and its suburbs, and we've been successful in a time where weekly papers have been tough to carve their niche," Ross said as Gillian listened with unwavering intent.

"Sounds like my guy's been putting his formidable mind to good use; and you're happy here."

"I am. I've got it all; now, that is. Great job, friends I'd walk through fire for. And now, I believe I'm the envy of every guy in San Diego—and everywhere else. I've got my very own girlfriend again," Ross kissed her gently as Gillian stroked his hair with her elegant fingers.

"This weekend has been quite the tumultuous one, in a nice way, for you—I won't lie and tell you I wouldn't like to find out about your friends, in due time. Your life's been turned inside out by me being here. I'll get to see your friends eventually. On your clock, though; not mine, OK?" Gillian understood, it seemed, the radical change that his world underwent. She was not just someone who ached to be filled, who displayed her passion for him in multiple, extremely satisfying ways, for both of them.

"Every time I think I've got you figured out, you reveal something different about yourself. I like that."

"You have a history, a past, a road map which you've followed. I'm making my own history as I go along." She snuggled a bit closer to the man whom she owed her life to as a work week unlike any other for Ross was mere hours away.

The fivesome who made up the heart of CityLife, for once, arrived at the same time at the Library Lofts in the near-center of town. It also doubled as retail space, and that's where the newspaper called home. Greene, Holm, McCall, Lloyd and Vincent car-pooled this Monday, and got there before their boss did.

"Thing is, folks, to let Will go at his own speed in unloading; we can't second-guess or anything like it, "Vincent reminded them. "He seemed spooked shitless on Friday. I'm worried about him."

"Me too," said Holm, "The important thing is to be there for him. Friends are what he needs most, especially now. He was in our corner when CityLife just started out and stuck with us."

"Now it's our turn to be there for him," McCall finished it as he fiddled for the keys. "So when he gets here, just be cool and stuff—"

When they open the door, they see donuts, bagels and coffee du jour in a spread on one of the few unoccupied tables, with a familiar face staring back at them.

"Happy Monday, gang; thought I'd beat you, time-wise, for a change. For once, a Monday which isn't your basic screw-this start of a week."

They were stunned. William Ross, already there; he usually comes in just before or just after them, but this looked like he was there for a little while before 9 AM.

"Will; this for us?" Greene wondered. "What's the occasion?"

"A turning of the corner this weekend, turning a new page, a new outlook. I had a pretty nice weekend, which is saying something."

"Wait one sec," Vincent noticed something in Ross' demeanor that he instantly picked up on. "You look like you forgot to add a 'new' to that list there."

"What?"

"A new . . . friend?"

Lloyd nodded knowingly. "A girlfriend? Really, Will?"

"Now hold on—"

"The classic giveaway," Holm chimed in, walking toward him, "You're a man of many talents, William, but fortunately, lying isn't one of them. It's a girl, and I'd wager a month's pay on it."

"Good for you—"

"What Rebecca said. You're gonna introduce us to her, aren't you?" McCall was already ahead of the rest of them.

"Time out, guys!" Ross pleaded; he was bombarded with interest from his friends on this reversal of fortune, for once, pleasant. "OK, it is a girl; you got me there. I now have faith in whomever said 'just go to the laundromat and you'll have a chance of finding somebody there as much as anywhere.' And I did."

"Uh huh; did you win her over with the 'look at me, I'm just a clueless guy who doesn't know jack shoot about how to operate these big-assed washers'?" Lloyd kidded him.

"Is it promising, Will?" Greene asked him, a look of concern on his grizzled face.

"You could say that."

"So how 'bout we meet her, check her out—" McCall asked as he finished his bagel.

"Yeah, give her the third, fourth and fifth degrees and shit," Vincent finished his thought.

"C'mon, guys, this isn't the Spanish frigging' inquisition here," Ross smiled back and finished his doughnut. "She's a bit shy, I think. Just a gut feeling. She's new to SD and she's just getting her bearings; been here for about 3 weeks. How about if I run it by her and if she signs off on it, we'll have dinner—on me—all of us. Deal?"

The foursome nodded approval and proceeded to wolf down the breakfast treats Ross had provided for them.

Chapter 9

"**S**hy?"

Later that evening, as they watched a movie, the raspy, throaty voice echoed through his apartment.

"Well, they were peppering me with questions right and left, so—"

"You said I was *shy*?" Gillian teased William as they shared a bag of popcorn while 'Field of Dreams' was playing on the television. "You know, Will, shyness wasn't exactly a factor—" she kissed him lovingly at this, "or an issue," another kiss, "when you shaped me, when you created me into what I am."

"OK, so shy may have been a tad inaccurate," he admitted sheepishly. "One thing led to another, and before I could get a syllable in edgewise, they're hot for meeting you."

"Sure," she said without a moment's hesitation.

"You certain about that? I was, sure, but this soon?"

"Why not?"

"Only because telling a fib will be, I daresay, somewhat necessary here. Your place of birth, shall we say, would cause something of a sensation, and lead them to think we were both 51 cards short of a full deck."

"Wouldn't it?" Gillian, ever the budding prankster, said with a wicked gleam in her eyes. "It would almost, but not quite, equal the look on your face the first day we officially were introduced.

"Don't worry, Will; a suitable cover story will pass muster with them by Friday. That OK with you, Friday? This will be one of the highlights of my arrival; to meet the people you call your co-workers; your second family, perhaps."

"They've been that of late. We're a pretty tight-knit group. I can't wait to show off the firecracker that you are, and that I can call my very own best-est friend. Friday it is, then. I think they'll like you. They'll have to take a number, though. I'm not letting anyone cut in on this line." Ross hugged her, his eyes swelling with tears, and he didn't know why.

"What's wrong? You OK?"

He took a moment to compose himself. "I've been OK since you came into my life, Gillian. I hope I've been a good guy-"

"None of that, Will. They don't make 'em like you anymore. And that's the loss of every girl who's ever crossed your path. Your creativity I can personally attest to. I love you, and I won't share you with anybody. You have no comprehension of how much you mean to me; you may think you know, but you have no idea."

"Watching MTV while I was gone from work, eh?" Ross quipped, flicking his eyes upward.

"Yep. And rewriting the record book on World Series 2k3."

"No way."

"Way, I'm afraid."

"I'll have to get a second controller so I can take you on head-to-head, and then we'll see who goes to school," he said with a playful tease in his voice.

"Bring it on, Ross."

Which he—and she—did. Eventually.

So the date was set. Gillian pretty much stayed around the house for the remainder of the week. She had food, a library of video games and 500 channels of satellite TV to occupy her time.

For Ross, his apprehension over the impending dinner, and the unveiling of his woman to his colleagues lessened, rather than increased. There were certain other realities that creeped in, though; realities that smacked him upside the head. Such as the knowledge Gillian could never hold a job of any sort because she had no background to speak of, and if she tried, someone may start asking questions and that would lead down a road of no return. Especially in these times where one which carries no ID nor can account for themselves can be in a world of trouble. He had enough of an income to never have her put in a position like that. Ross didn't spend money like a drunken sailor, neither in his youth or his adulthood. He invested wisely in the stock market, cutting his losses when he had to, and buying when he felt the time was right. He wasn't spared the dot-bomb bust at the end of the century, but it didn't wipe him out, either.

He was happy.

Friday came and went for the most part, save for a 7:45PM reservation at the Star of the Sea restaurant, at Harbor Drive and Ash Street, which serves up a spectacular view of San Diego Bay. He changed at work and drove home, thinking Gillian would be ready when he got there.

6:30 came, and he walked into the apartment, and no sign of his beloved. "Gillian; you here?"

No answer. He looked in the bedroom; nothing; he scanned the rest of the apartment, and she was nowhere around. Did she forget about it? Maybe she wandered off for some reason. Ross was getting increasingly concerned.

"Gillian? Please tell me you're just jerking my chain a bit—"

"Heart racing yet?"

She emerged from the bathroom—duh, he never checked there—in a stunning white velvet dress with spaghetti straps, a black miniskirt, black shoes with three-inch high heels which contrasted brilliantly with her golden legs. Ross was paralyzed with wonder; he literally could not stop staring at her.

"I'll take that as a vote of confidence on my outfit," Gillian said, knowing full well she floored him with it. "Ready?"

"As I'll ever be, G." He held her hands and kissed them, and then wrapped his long arms around her. "You look dangerous tonight."

"I *am* dangerous," she replied, kissing him repeatedly for a half-minute. "OK, I'm not dangerous, but I had you goin', right?"

William nodded as he opened the door to let them out, and toward a meeting each looked forward to.

Chapter 10

The five of them arrived at Star of the Sea within a few minutes of each other. There was a buzz among the group as they waited for the guests of honor to arrive.

"I didn't think he'd plunge in this soon, but now that we know he has a girlfriend, it seems to have settled him down a lot," McCall offered his assessment. "In hindsight, that is."

"Anybody seen her with him so we know what we're looking for?" Lloyd was understandably curious.

"I don't have a clue," Vincent added as they waited to get into the restaurant. "It's good he's back in circulation. There's been a change in his outlook; for the better, I add. You noticed it?"

"Like night and day," Holm took off her coat and gave it to the person responsible for checking all the outerwear. "Whoever it is deserves a pat on the back for bringing him back from the brink . . . hello."

They weren't alone any longer. William and a luminous Gillian were in their midst; nobody could speak for a few seconds, so stunned they were collectively by her incredible beauty.

"Sorry about the delay; got caught in traffic a bit; still made it, though. Brian, Dan, Rebecca, Barry, Amy—this is Gillian, my girlfriend."

"It's a genuine pleasure to meet all of you finally; he's always talking about his Fab Five," she shook the hands of each of them.

I've been waiting for this for a week; any friend of William is one of mine, too."

"Reservation for 7, party's name is Ross." he walked over to the maitre'd who escorted them to their luxurious and roomy table located near a window which looked out on San Diego Bay. After they settled in and got their menus, Dan began the questioning which Ross—and her—knew was coming.

"I detect a Canadian accent there; you from there?"

"Was it that much a giveaway?" she smiled. "I arrived here a few weeks ago from Winnipeg; got tired a bit of the cold weather and decided to come to where it was a bit warmer. I decided to extend my vacation a few extra weeks and you have a great city here."

They ordered dinner, each of them, then resumed. "You're a bit on the young side-"

"Amy!"

"It's OK, Will; I am young. Twenty-five, actually. William is the first boyfriend I've had. I didn't think guys like him existed. I was wrong. In the time I've known him, I'm learning new stuff left and right. And to find out he's available? It's my good fortune, then."

Ross blushed a moment later. Gillian was taking the conversation point and not showing any sign of tentativeness. Goddamn, this lady is off the meter, he thought to himself. No friggin' fear at all.

"I've had months of experience with mastering the intricacies of laundromat stuff," he said, "and you can now count me in as a believer that it is an underrated place for meeting women. Not that I was looking that day; she just showed up; she was just there. Maybe my mom and dad were right."

"What about?" Gillian looked at him soulfully.

"Sometimes when you stop looking for love, it finds you. It finds you on its terms and time, not yours."

On that tender note, the dinners they ordered were ready and waiting to be wolfed down. Afterward, Ross's friends resumed their inquisition of his companion.

"So what did you do in Winnipeg?" McCall began this round of questioning.

"I was a graduate student at Manitoba College. Was thinking about going to Simon Fraser U. out in Vancouver, but decided it was a bit too far away. Got a Bachelor of Arts in psychology and minored in film studies. Nothing of what you all are doing, but it's made me a well-rounded person. With the economy the way it is, however, things were a little slow, and I guess the film-studying side of me emerged more, it turned out. I'm fascinated by creating stuff; from the mind's eye to reality. That's what movies are. A different reality, true, but when you envision something and then have it emerge for all to see, it gives you such a rush of power, of something good and pure."

"And a vision that's all one's own; sometimes," Greene added, "Have you gotten anything off the ground yet?"

"I've been here just three weeks, so nothing yet. But there's a whole city and new people to observe, to study. And a friend to turn to," Gillian reached over and took Ross' hand and held it.

"What about family? Do you have any back home?" Amy wondered.

"I did; past tense. Both my parents died in a car accident when I was 20. So I've been on my own, pretty much since then. I had no family to fall back on until I met William."

"How did you cope?"

Gillian took a bit of time and searched her boyfriend's eyes for an answer. Perhaps she didn't expect that question to be asked. Ross' insides tensed up. He daren't show any panic, however.

"I never quit believing that things wouldn't get better. And they got a whole lot better when he came into my life."

Ross exhaled. Nice save, G . . .

"At the risk of turning my date's face a permanent shade of red," Gillian continued, "William's told me of the bond you guys have, like a family. Seeing you here, and grilling me like any best friends should, I know that he's chosen his friends well." She grinned, knowing what they were up to all the time.

"A toast, then," Greene raised his wine glass. "To Gillian; we're tight, the six of us. You're OK in my book. You rebounded from a bad hand life dealt you and you landed on your feet."

"Here here," McCall said. Each of them raised their glasses to their guest. Vincent and Holm, however, raised theirs a little slower than the rest of them. "Thanks, Will, for this dinner; it's been terrific."

"No sweat, really," he shot a knowing glance at Gillian who made his insides sweat multiple bullets.

"How about we work this meal off," Gillian suggested. There's a nightclub we passed by, Buffalo Joe's that I saw on TV a bit earlier; it gave it a pretty good review. It's only a few minutes away."

"Night's still young, guys," Ross said as the check was delivered and he paid for it with his credit card. "Whaddaya say?"

"Why not? You can show the rest of 'em what I already know—you're a hella dancer," Gillian said matter-of-factly.

That elicited shocked looks from the dinner party. "Really, Will?" Vincent said.

"Yeah, like put all the pressure on me now, Gillian," Ross said. She sure liked living dangerously; his dancing skills had improved, only he didn't show them off; now that he thought about it, he never put himself in a position since he came out here that he danced the night away.

"Count us in; this night just got a lot more interesting." McCall seemed to speak for the majority of them, smiling like a guy who knew something was about to happen before anyone else did.

Chapter 11

Buffalo Joe's, about a half-hour later.

The place is packed with party goers; it's a pretty tight fit, but the seven of them manage to get inside, and it's not long afterward that Gillian and William do ease on over to the dance floor and begin what they've done in both realities of theirs—imagined and real—they cut quite the rug as a techno-dance number plays in the background.

Among his coworkers, shock is the overriding emotion.

"She's 25?" Vincent shook his head as he sipped a cocktail at the bar. "I never knew he'd go for someone so young."

"Gillian seems on the up and up," McCall rebutted. "She's a firecracker, that's for damned sure. It was almost as if she was expecting to get grilled."

"You think William tipped her off?" Holm suggested. "I don't know about any of you, but she seems a bit too perfect. Too ordinary. Call it intuition-"

"It's not just a woman's thing this time," Vincent cut in. "Did you see how she hesitated when Amy asked how Gillian coped after her parents' deaths? It was almost as if she didn't know what to say, as if she—"

"C'mon, Brian, I don't sense any bad karma," Greene begged to differ as he fidgeted on his barstool. "She turned out OK, and he seems so happy with her. They look like they belong together. And after what he's been through, at least let him have some time to salve his wounds."

Amy Lloyd concurred. "Yeah, she's almost young enough to be his daughter; ask Celine Dion how much of a detriment that is. We're talking' a quarter-century there. And Ally McBeal keeping up with the Jones—bordering on 30? I think we can make allowances for 14 years; and what the heck is the problem? Love is a gift. It doesn't know any age."

"Except if you're Anna Nicole and marry some guy 60 years her senior who happens to be a gazillionaire," McCall pointed out to a round of laughs, "For Love or Money would have had a field day with that one."

"We just don't want to see him on the wrong end of heartache again," Vincent said, backing up Holm's reluctance to embrace his new girlfriend. "We don't even know her last name."

They looked at the two of them, who eventually became the center of attention as they continued to tear it up as the music played.

"Who the Christ knew he could dance like that?" McCall's eyes were glazed over in astonishment. "Didn't picture him as a contestant for American Bandstand."

"Who knew he danced, period?" Greene corrected him. "She's quite good, however. Dangerously good."

Maybe it was the way he said it, but that touched a spark of concern with the two who seemed the most uneasy about Gillian. The couple returned to where they left the others, a bit pooped out, but still feeling chipper.

"Not bad, Will; not bad at all," Gillian commended her partner.

"It's nice to show off a side of me that I don't usually reveal," he turned introspective for a moment, realizing that this was the first time he ever let his guard down in a manner like this. "I'm sorry for keeping that part of me on the sidelines from you all."

"You had the courage to show it at all," Lloyd stepped toward him, speaking for them all. "Don't let that part of you be a stranger, OK? And Gillian—"

"Yeah, we didn't get your last name," Vincent asked, seizing the moment.

"Moore; Gillian Moore," smiling without hesitation and nodded her head toward him.

"Gillian, thanks for coming into his life," Lloyd resumed, "He's a good person, and . . ." she wavered on telling her about what had happened in the recent past, and then thought better of it, "Now we can learn some new dance moves from him."

Ross exhaled at that point. He looked at her a long moment; thanks for not spilling the beans about what happened, he thought to himself.

They spent the next hour or two dancing, drinking and chatting before they all called it a night.

"That was exhilarating!"

Gillian rolled over and snuggled closer to William, now both back in his apartment, after their revelry ended about 2 AM.

"*You* were exhilarating back there," Ross corrected her, kissing her gently, calmly. "That was a little past my bedtime, but it was worth it. It was a privilege to see you work," Ross joked, stroking her perfect black hair. "The confidence you showed, the assuredness. I'm not certain I would have pulled it off under the same circumstances."

"Shit, you would have, Will. I came from inside you. The confidence I showed was already there, in your soul from the start. It was natural to tap into that. Although I did get thrown for a loop a tiny bit when Amy asked how I coped with my 'loss of family.'"

"Speak for oneself," Ross playfully scolded her, taking his hand and rolling it down her left arm. "I had major heartbeat skippage at that point. Nice Bernie Parent-esque save, however."

"It was intoxicating, William, to take their best shots. Your friends grilled me good, I will say that. But I realize it's only because they care. I sensed they wanted to protect you; from what, I don't know. I may have come from your idea of what your textbook companion is, but there are still some things I don't know about you. In time, I guess. Like you were hurt, deeply—and they just wanted to make sure you wouldn't get hurt again."

Ross thought about that; if she only knew. But she won't. Not if he could help it. "Like Brian said, we're pretty tight, the six of us.

I also felt it, you're right. I assure you, sweetheart, there's no hurt. Only joy. And I've been wallowing in it from the moment I saw you. You've changed my life, G; the darkness is gone. I love you; body, mind and soul."

Gillian shook her head approvingly. "Sweetheart, huh? We've taken our relationship to the next level; the point where lovey-dovey names start replacing our own on occasion, a few times at first, and then increasing exponentially, darling."

"Yeah, hun," Ross kept the wordplay going, "I'm gonna like this."

"Long may we reign, Will," she purred as they finally retired for the night, reveling in the silence, the peacefulness of the night. After all, she came from the night and he's on his way back from it.

Chapter 12

Gillian and William bummed the whole weekend, just staying close to home, and went on a moviegoing spree. They did their duty in breaking in with his inner circle; this weekend would be theirs alone. Romantic comedies, dramas, sci-fi, escapist fare. And for once, no wild, window-rattling lovemaking. They indulged in the basic, raw passion they shared, but it also evolved. It became something more—a relationship as traditional and as strong as any between two people who care about and love each other.

In only a month of being together, they were on their way to becoming soul mates. Sadly, something as inevitable as a sunrise intruded on them, William especially, which ensured they would be torn apart.

Monday.

Brian Vincent told his wife that he needed to do some research on a project at work, and that he would be visiting the San Diego public library's Central Branch. Yes, it was a Saturday, but they still had normal business hours, 9:30 in the morning until 5:30 at night.

He went to the second floor computer lab where a free spot for a computer beckoned him. Vincent began his surfing at the Google website, plugging in a name.

"Gillian Moore."

Ten pages of search results answered. This was going to take a while . . .

About an hour later, Vincent looked at the last web page that the engine brought up. He scratched his head and looked down at his notepad, one which was empty. There was no record of her on this website. So he switched to plan B, the Manitoba College website, where he got the main phone number of it, as well as the Winnipeg Police Department, and then left. His next stop would be back home, where he would probably rack up a good-sized phone bill.

No picture of her, no trace of where she came from, no family. Surely that would change once Brian went the old-school route in getting information; the telephone.

Another week begins.

She was still asleep when the snooze button kicked in for the last time, at 9:30 AM. That woke Gillian up, finally. She looked around to see if William was still there, and when she turned to the right side, a pocket cassette recorder answered, with the words "play me" written on a yellow post-it note. Gillian followed the advice.

"Hey, sweetie; you were really zonked out after our movie binge yesterday—maybe it was some leftover from Friday. Anybody can just write a note letting them know they've gone for work while their better half is still sleeping—and looking as spectacular as ever. I'm at work, missing you every instant along the way. Go wild for breakfast and lunch. Make yourself whatever you feel you can. Shouldn't be too much overtime today, so I'll be home regular, pretty much. I'll try and call later to see how you are, and to hear that voice of voices. I miss you and I love you, Gillian. Bye."

For the first time since she was a part of his world, the tears flowed down Gillian's cheeks; it was unorthodox, it was left-field, and it was wonderful. She mouthed 'I love you too, Will' as she walked out of his bedroom into the main area of his studio apartment. About a half-hour later she enjoyed a cheese omelet, the breakfast meal of choice when he took her out on their first official 'date.'

A little bit later, instead of playing video games and watching

TV, she instead decided to try out his burgeoning collection of books, which was across the room where the stereo system was. She read a collection of sportswriting stories first; couldn't put it down, actually. Gillian discovered another trait she shared with Ross—both had a voracious appetite for reading. When she was done that, she next picked up Glenn Kleier's spectacular millennium thriller "The Last Day," about a modern day potential Messiah who may or may not be the catalyst for Armageddon, when something fluttered out of a back page in the book and fell to the floor. Gillian noticed it and picked it up.

It was a picture of William. With another woman.

It looked like it was outside a church. It looked like they were very much in love. She didn't know what to make of it; surely that was in the past, and a check of the back of the photo provided a time stamp of when the picture was developed. It was about six weeks ago. But before she could figure out what she was feeling, something caught her eye on a table close by.

A flashing red light. His answering machine.

Could he have called already, and I was so caught up in the book that I missed it?, she wondered. Gillian walked tentatively over to the phone. She wasn't that sure about how to use the machine, so she pushed a button, hoping for the best to hear him. There would be some explaining for him to do when he got home . . .

Chapter 13

5:35 PM.

A knock on the door. Gillian briskly walks over to the peephole to check who it is before she opens it.

"Hi," William kissed her and walked inside. "I'm sorry I didn't get a chance to call. Things were busy; it's the day before our next issue goes to press and that's always a bugger to get . . . what's that smell?"

She motioned over to the kitchen. "I'm doing the dinner honors tonight; I wanted to be more useful around here, so steaks are on the menu in a few, OK?"

"That was nice of you, Gillian; anything happen while I was gone?"

She ignored the question and casually walked over to his answering machine and pressed the play button.

"Sorry I didn't get you before you left, Will; it's Brian. I won't be coming in today, as I'm a bit under the weather. Maybe it's just as well; don't be pissed that I did this, but I did some checking last night, and I couldn't find any records of a "Gillian Moore" anywhere; Yahoo!, Google, Manitoba College dot edu. Jack shit. I can't risk going over your place as you may have her over there for a date. Meet me in Balboa Park tonight around 9, OK? The Visitors

Center. Something's fishy here, Will. It may be nothing, but after what you've been through, better to be mad at me for nothing than to be happy and not say anything and have you go through grief cubed. I'll see you then, and tomorrow I'll try to make it in."

Ross is speechless, stunned beyond words.

"He suspects *something*, Will. From his tone, it doesn't sound like his investigation is going to conclude anytime soon, either."

"He never called work," Ross noted, trying to find out if he did. "He didn't tell anybody else about it. Maybe because we don't have any individual offices per se, we're all where we can see one another that he didn't want to tip any of the others off. This is very unlike him, Gill."

"Apropos word, cause I'm beginning to unlike this guy. I'm scared, Will; I don't officially exist, remember? What if he takes it further and others get nosy? People without a past or proof of who they are tends to be somewhat frowned upon these days. I don't think you need to be reminded of that."

No, he didn't, he thought to himself. Gillian may be a baby in chronological age, but she has knowledge of the world to spare. He took her hands and drew her close. "The absolute last thing I want is to put you in any danger. I'll straighten out Brian tonight and nip this square in the bud, from your lips to God's ears."

"Well, you already know my opinion of you on the latter part of that." Gillian wrapped her arms around him as Ross winced at that; even if in a minuscule part of his mind came to the conclusion that she may be in fact, right.

"Let's eat."

After, the two passed the time enjoying viewing the first season of the classic television series "Sports Night" on his DVD player. It was William's favorite show; he recognized the quality and excellence that oozed from every area; the writing, the directing, the acting, the lack of a laugh track. It was in this serene moment that Gillian pulled something out of her pocket and showed it to him.

"Will . . . who is this lady?"

His world stopped.

The color drained from William's face once more, much like

the moment he saw Gillian for real. Only this time, he was the one who was shocked beyond belief. He got up and kept looking at the picture.

"I thought I got rid of all of these . . ." he muttered.

"You didn't answer me; who is she? Besides your girlfriend—"

"It's not like that, Gillian," he sharply replied. He was in a daze now; Ross looked like he'd just been told his parents died.

"It was outside a church 6 weeks ago. Six weeks. I never pictured you as someone who'd cheat on—"

"That's not true; let it be. She's a distant memory."

"Distant?" Gillian dug in her heels, figuratively. "She was a bookmark in one of the novels you have. Not too distant, if you ask me."

"A lot can change in 6 weeks; less than that. Please trust me and accept my promise that she's not in my life anymore, and . . ." he was on the verge of crying at this point and turned away from her.

"What aren't you telling me, Will? For God's sake, we've given of ourselves to one another, given and received love in its rawest form. I've been honest with you, and goddammit, it's got to be a two-way street—"

"Because she nearly destroyed my life, that's why!" he exploded, shouting at Gillian as if she was an enemy. "I can't relive that again; don't ask me to, G; I'm begging you."

Gillian had touched a nerve with the power of a third rail on an elevated train line; it was that searing. She abruptly switched from confrontation to conciliation. "William, you're still not over her yet. You can't keep it bottled up in you; do you understand? I happen to think the world of you, but you've got to face this down and deal so you can move on; that *we* can move on. It's obvious you've never gotten to the point of talking about it; not even with your friends, perhaps, yet. Who is this woman, and why does she torture you still?"

Her words sliced through his mind-numbing pain as easily as one would step over a crack in the sidewalk. Ross' psyche needed that boost. He sat back down.

"Let me tell you a story of the cruelty that people are sometimes capable of."

A tenseness ensued as William Ross prepared to take Gillian on a guided tour of his recent life prior to their introduction. A quirk that she didn't know about it already, since his memories of that time resided in the same place she came from—his mind. Nevertheless, she had no idea; maybe he subconsciously guarded that all too well.

"You're right, Gillian; I never dealt with it, not with anyone. I was going to tell my other friends, but some visitor who dropped by at a certain laundromat put that on hold indefinitely," he smiled ruefully toward her.

"I'm here, and I'm listening, Will. No judgments, you have my word."

He drew in his breath and let out a sharp exhale, steeling himself for the road ahead.

"Her name was Sarah."

Chapter 14

TWO YEARS AGO . . .

The Doubletree Club San Diego hotel was where the official party to celebrate CityLife's anointment as Southern California's most read weekly newspaper was held. Its parent company organized the event, where Ross's staff—McCall, Vincent, Holm, Lloyd and Alison Kendall, the then-entertainment writer were among the guests. Ross was still assistant editor then. Barry Greene was not yet hired by the paper. There were about 150 people in the banquet hall as the parent company's CEO took the microphone.

"We are here today to celebrate the renaissance of CityLife; three years ago, it was on the verge of going under. Thanks to Bob and William and the staff here tonight, we've risen from the ashes to become the most trusted and read weekly newspaper in all of SoCal. And we're not that far away from being the #1 weekly newspaper in the most populous state in the Union. With the quality we have here, I don't see that as an unreasonable goal. We've got a weekend of rest, and enjoy the fruits—and liquids—" laughter there, "of the evening!"

A round of applause followed as the staff, the advertisers and their friends who were invited to this exclusive party could get down to the business of unwinding after a journey which has been successful so far. Roger Atkinson, the owner of CityLife, forty-ish slowly walked over to where Ross and his inner circle were talking.

"I wanted to thank you personally for the work ethic you all brought to the table; an editor is only as good as the people he hires, and by that reckoning, I'm going to leave this paper in most capable hands."

"Leave the paper? What do you mean?" Vincent asked.

"I've been tended a job offer up in Sacramento. It's nearer to my family, and I already told the executive board that I'm accepting their offer—and that I recommended you, Will, to take my place as editor."

Ross was shell shocked; he, nor anyone else had any idea that was coming. "Mr. Atkinson, I don't know what to say . . . you showed me the ropes since I've been here—"

"You've proved to me and the executive board that you're ready to take us to the proverbial next level; I can leave knowing the paper is in good hands," Atkinson shook Ross' hand and hugged him. He left them to talk among themselves.

"Wow, Will; congratulations deluxe; you certainly earned it," Alison was the first of his staff to say. "You didn't have any idea, did you?"

"Nope. None. The only reason why I'm at where I'm at is because I've got good people working for me—and with me. I feel kind of bad that one of you didn't get the chance, and now I've got a decision to make on who's going to be my second in charge." Ross was a bit down at that prospect; he didn't know why he said it out loud, to all of the prospective candidates. "I won't go outside, that's for damn sure. You have my word on that."

"Thanks for that," Holm replied. Now that's something you don't see often; a boss promising to promote from within. "We don't have anything to worry about."

"I don't know about you, but how's about a round—on me?" Ross pitched that idea, which needless to say got unanimous approval from his five friends. He left them and walked toward the open bar, a bit stunned, still, from the news of his promotion. He turned around to see where his friends were; when he turned back—

Splash!

He had bumped into someone who had a drink in their hand and it went flying. "I'm so sorry, I wasn't looking where—"

He couldn't believe his eyes. A woman more beautiful than he could have possibly imagined, but just a little bit perturbed at this particular moment.

"We need a traffic light at this intersection," she joked, the British accent music to his ears. "I will have to see your drivers' license, of course."

"My fault all around . . ." his voice trailed off. Ross could not stop looking at her eyes, as if compelled to by a higher power. Red hair, almost, but not quite as tall as him, with perfectly crafted cheekbones, white teeth and just the right shape of lips.

"What, you never seen a girl before, have you?," she suggested. "The least you can do after walking into me is to tell me who you are."

He still couldn't get over how beautiful she looked, but knew he had to say something. "I'm William Ross, assistant editor of the CityLife newspaper here in San Diego. And you are?"

"Assistant editor, huh? I just came over here from England and I must say I'm impressed; you could improve on your football coverage, though."

"We cover the Chargers enough; a bit too good for their liking, and I knew all along you were talking about the football practiced by 99.99% of the rest of the world," he joked, feeling more at ease by the moment. "What club are you a fan of?"

"West Ham United. I get up at 6:30 AM on match days to watch their games at the only pub who's willing to have the TV on that early."

Ross screwed his face quizzically. The lady sensed he did not share her loyalty to it.

"Let me guess; a ManU fan, right?"

"The best United there is right now."

She sighed audibly. "Please; they're the Yankees of football over there; think they can buy every good player. There's a reason why we have fans with A.B.M. t-shirts; anyone but Man U," she sighed, now perhaps regretting their chance meeting. "That's strike one."

"Hey, now; I can't help what team I root for; how are you related to CityLife that you're here tonight?"

"I work in the insurance business, for the company that owns your paper."

"Cool; but I didn't get your name," he prodded her once more.

"That's cause I didn't give it yet," she smiled. "You're an eager bloke, I'll give you that."

"Well, I just needed a name so I could find out where to send the money order to for the new dress you'll need thanks to my not looking where I was going."

"You know what, Mr. Ross; you're not a good liar," the woman replied, "That would be a second strike . . . normally."

"Well, I don't smoke or do drugs, either, so that's four strikes then; I'm honest to a fault most times; like in the need to take off the gloves and go after people who pose a threat to the civilized world; that reality television sucks big donkey dung, that everyone, no matter how damaged, deserves a chance at love, and that piercing one's body is not my thing."

She mulled it over for a minute. "Looks like we've got differences and similarities; at any rate, I've got to go; it was nice bumping, literally, into you."

Ross's face betrayed panic; here was this incredibly beautiful woman who was about to leave his life for good. "Go? You just got here, perhaps; I don't know your name, don't even know how to get in touch with you."

She turned around and smiled, then walked back toward him. "Don't fret, William; I'll find you. Besides, I now have one extra thing about me that I can tell you—next time."

Her eyes met his for a briefest moment to make sure he realized what had just happened, then she left, and left in her wake a man who felt like someone who had just had a life sentence commuted and moreso, pardoned. Ross's gaze followed her all the way out the door, a fact not lost on someone who had quietly walked up to him.

"Please answer this for me—did you at least get her name?" Dan McCall asked.

"Yeah," Ross replied. "She's the one.

The one, Dan."

On the other side of the room, someone else noticed the scene which unfolded, while she was getting something to eat. Where Alison Kendall suddenly turned sad-eyed. As with Dan and William, someone else was nearby.

"Alison, don't worry about it; if anything," Amy told her flat-out, "This is your chance to *tell him*. Don't let it slip through your fingers."

"I know, Amy; it's like I always get tongue-tied around him. He's such a nice guy, but I don't know if he feels for me the same way. And if I tell him and he says no, he's got somebody else . . ."

"You'll never know until you force the issue. Don't wait until it's too late. If you like him, let him know." Amy put a comforting hand on Alison's shoulder. "Carpe diem, Alison."

She'd tell him tomorrow. As good a time as any, she thought . . .

Chapter 15

The next day, Ross' emotions were on a roller coaster ride; he was the new editor of CityLife, but all he could think about (since the promotion would kick in the following month) was the woman he encountered at the party. It was all he could think about for every waking moment; on the drive home, when he began to fall asleep, when he had breakfast, and now.

It had been a year and change since his last relationship with a 30-something woman; as it turned out, she was a closet lesbian, of all things. He found out by accident. Maybe that luck would change. He made some phone calls near the end of the day, trying to find out who exactly it was who enchanted him so, to no avail.

A knock on the door of his office yielded Brian Vincent. "Hey, Will, someone's here for their 4:15PM meeting with you."

"I don't remember a 4:15 with anyone; I'm pushing 40, but I don't think I'm absent-minded yet," he chuckled. Before Vincent said anything else, the subject of the appointment came into view. Ross' jaw nearly dropped to the floor.

"Hello, Mr. Ross; you were expecting me, right? If not I can leave—"

In his office was the woman he saw from the party. In faded blue jeans and a pink cutoff top which showed her trim, lean midsection. It was all he could do to not hug her right then and there.

"Yes, I am going cuckoo; I've been expecting you, Miss—"

"Sarah Jenkins," she offered her hand, which Ross took gingerly. "It's a pleasure to finally, officially, make your acquaintance."

"Thanks, Brian, that's all." After he left, he continued to look at her, silently thanking the gods for answering his prayers. They agreed to a dinner date after work that day. As they were leaving, someone else just came into the office from an assignment. Alison was crestfallen as William and Sarah walked by, oblivious to everyone and everything except each other.

She was just too late; the Fates gave her their answer, she knew that now.

William and Sarah went to Buffalo Joe's restaurant for their first sit-down dinner date. The place is quiet for a Thursday; not too many people around yet for 6PM.

"Clichéd as this will sound, what's a woman like you doing 7,000 miles from home?" Ross asked, as he looked over the menu.

"Got tired of the wet weather and decided to move to somewhere warm; my mum and dad have some friends of theirs out here, and loved it so much they decided to stay. That was last year. It was tough leaving London, but I've settled in at SDSU—San Diego State, and have a job at the parent company of your paper.

"I've been there a year, already; half on an internship, and now full-time. I'm in the marketing division. Last night was the first party I've been to in a while; a memorable one. Now you have a shot at redeeming yourself for your suspect taste in football teams," Sarah said, a mischievous grin forming on her lips.

"Jealousy is never pretty, even though you are," he shot right back.

"Please, you Yanks can't even get the name right; it's football. It's not FISA; Federation of International Soccer Associations, but FIFA."

"C'mon, Sarah, you're preaching to the choir here; it's just that whenever your national team goes, it's 'hide the women and children, the hooligans are in the house.'"

"True, but we're trying to improve things . . . so what the heck is wrong with reality television shows? Notice I'm doing a point-by-point critique of the things you said you didn't like last night, which I do," Sarah teased him as she sipped a diet coke while they were waiting for their dinner.

"Reality TV is proof positive Newton Minow was right with his 'TV is a vast wasteland' comment before you were born." Ross began, "Yes, you too can now humiliate yourself, to be exposed as shallow, conniving, clueless and a poster child for 12 month continuous education. And millions of people will see you do it. It's the creative equivalent of striking your flag and running up a bed sheet with the phrase 'No mas!' written on it." He was in full rant mode now, even though his voice was calm and level. "Television can be and sometimes is a medium which has no peers. Just remove the 'rs' from that, and that's reality TV in a nutshell, and what it does to anyone unfortunate enough to watch it these days."

"Wow . . . don't sugarcoat your opinions, William, please," Jenkins gently kidded him as dinner was now served.

"It was OK at first; there were a few good shows, but anymore it's just total . . . what's your word for B.S.?"

"Bollocks."

He momentarily lost his train of thought. "I love how you say that," he stated without thinking. He blushed noticeably and Sarah tried to stifle a tender smile at that.

"Your honesty is refreshing. Now if I may be equally so; your country, using your constitution as birdcage-lining these days against the most heinous threat to civilization since Hitler. There are rules in war, William, and your boss man is losing more friends and allies than he's winning."

"The only rule these demons abide, Sarah, is that there's no rules except kill yourself and take as many innocents as you can with you. It's a different world we live in now, and whenever the enemy is thwarted because things are done faster or when shortcuts were made to find out what was about to go down, then I daresay the end justifies the means. Yes, it runs counter to what we are. I respectfully say if it's either us or them, I vote us."

"But you forget the words of one of your own founders; 'those who sacrifice freedom for security deserve neither freedom nor security.' You're on a slippery slope, you Yanks. I worry for you as a country. We've stood side by side with you when everyone else waffled. Just be careful of the path you take. Because once you're committed to it, there's no way back."

He nodded. Perhaps they were in agreement more than either of them realized.

"On a lighter note, I am young enough to be your daughter."

Ross' face was frozen in disbelief. Where the heck did that come from?

"Come again?"

"It was going to come up sooner or later, so I figured I'd get it out of the way now," Sarah said. "I'll admit, I'm flattered you think highly of me, but the inescapable fact is that I am fully half your age. I need you to know that I'm concerned about it. You are the oldest man I've ever had dinner with who's not my dad."

"Hey now, I'm not 40," Ross protested. "I'm 39.95 . . . plus tax."

That created a smile on Sarah's face. He seized on that.

"Sarah, I'm not a guy who's looking to recapture his youth. I've had a good youth, and a good pre-middle age. But when I saw you last night, it wouldn't have mattered if you were 18, 28 or 58. There is a quality about you that has stirred my soul. For all your doubts, I think the fact you're here tonight with me says something. That you want to go on this journey with me, side-by-side. You would have disappeared and not come back if you weren't. I hope to God you're not spoken for, Sarah—and I promise you I will treat you with the respect you deserve. I do like you. That I can't deny; not to you, not to myself. Honest to a fault I am. And I want to see you again. If you'll have me."

She pondered it for a moment. Sarah was here, seeing him a second time. Every instinct she had told her to pause and see where the chips fell. She knew he was instantly smitten by her. And their lively back-and-forth had been exhilarating. Sarah drew in her breath.

"No."

It was exactly what he didn't need to hear. Dammit. This hurts.

"No, I'm not spoken for. At least not until a moment ago, Will."

Now it was his turn to be utterly shocked to his socks. "You mean . . ."

"Was that good, in terms of a swerve? Had you going there, didn't I?" she reached over and held his hands in hers. "Tell me more about yourself, William Ross.

"And from this moment, consider yourself my boyfriend."

The rest of the dinner (and subsequent dancing) were more than Ross could have hoped. It was about 12 midnight when he took her home, which was in the Mission Valley neighborhood of town. Now the goal here would be to not mess it up for the future, whatever that would be.

"That was one of the better evenings I've had in a long time, Sarah; you are an exceptional woman to be around."

"You're not too bad yourself," they're at the doorstep of her house. "You've done all the right things, Will. I had a lovely evening, too. I've dated guys in the past and you're the first one who didn't look like all he wanted to do was shag me."

Again, Sarah had a penchant for leaving him speechless, mouth open in amazement. Nothing was off limits for her, opinion-wise. "I admit the thought crossed my mind more than a few times tonight. The next moment, I said to myself, there's a time and a place for all things. Being intimate with you falling into that category." he squeezed her hands ever-so-gently.

"Why, Will, do you want to shag me?" Sarah said playfully, her face just inches from his, her sweet perfume doing a number on his sense of smell, as in terrific-smelling. He realized this was a proverbial fork-in-the-road moment.

"I want more nights like this; more days to look forward to thinking about the next time I see you. There will come a time to . . . shag," a sheepish grin emerged from Ross at this point, "This isn't a one-nighter. Down the road, maybe, and only when or if you think it's time. But now now. I'm sorry, Sarah."

She nodded—and then kissed him unexpectedly, Ross returning the kindness, his answer received in spades. "So when will I see you again, Will?"

"How about lunch tomorrow? Or dinner? My social calendar is open, but I plan to fill it to overflowing before long," William embraced her tenderly and kissed Sarah flush on the lips, then walked to his car for the ride home to his condo. Returning home with the knowledge that he could build on this, knowing that his future is now officially brighter than the sun.

Chapter 16

"You do have a thing for younger women, Will," Gillian said matter-of-factly.

"One day, about 8 months into our relationship, Sarah said 'I love you' out of the blue, I followed with a similar declaration, and we both were officially an item. Her parents gave me all the degrees, and I don't mean college, either, that one grills a potential mate with and vice versa. Not long afterward, I proposed to her. Sarah said yes, and the wedding would have been 7 weeks from this Saturday."

"Would have been?"

"Yes; the bridal shower, the bachelor party, and all the trappings that mark the passage into couplehood came and went. Rehearsals at the church, which is where that particular picture came from. I was going to be married to The One. We all have The One; so I've been told, that is. Well, almost everyone.

"Wedding day arrives. All the staff from CityLife, my mom and dad flying in from Philly to see it," the tears flow unchecked down his face by now. "And now that that's out of the bag, you can put two and two together, only it wasn't two that day—"

"Jesus, no," Gillian instantly knew what he was about to say and spared him from saying it himself. "She left you at the altar."

He had to take a few moments to compose himself; Lord knows how he looked to her right about now. "It turns out the night before she cleaned out her apartment without anyone knowing it, and left a note with the landlord as she left. She got cold feet, basically. Sarah was afraid she would wind up like her family—divorced. She wrote that she 'did me a favor' by walking away."

"'Did you a favor'? What a bitch . . ."

"I can't fathom how you could devote two years out of one's life to someone, and then be afraid to take the final step and doesn't have the stones to tell you why she left you in the lurch. To love someone that much, that long and just end it. I don't have clue one as to where she is nor do I want to find out. I thought I closed the page on Sarah. I was wrong . . ." Ross couldn't hold the dam-sized amount of tears he had kept hidden since that fateful day and poured his heart out, burying his head in Gillian's shoulder and bawled.

"Get rid of the pain, Will; it's poisoned your very soul," Gillian hugged him back for all she was worth, and more. "I will never, NEVER, let another person inflict such pain on you; I swear it." She gently, gingerly maneuvered him into a position where he could rest comfortably, stretched out on the couch, massaging his forehead all the while, soothing his anguish. It seemed to calm him down and he mooched onto the couch to get a better position to rest a while.

With this shattered evening came a newfound resolve; Gillian decided that her own well-being was secondary to that of the man who brought her into the light of our world; a man whose darkest secret lay naked for her to see.

'Seeing' would be the operative word. She looked at his clock radio and 8:55 PM replied.

Perfect timing, Gillian thought . . .

8:56 PM.

Brian Vincent had arrived at Balboa Park and was heading in the direction of the Visitors Center; there was some traffic, so he was slightly late for his meeting with Ross. As he walked through the park, he felt a gust of wind behind him. Strong enough to pique his curiosity if anyone was behind him, so he turned around to see. Yet no one was around within 15 yards of him. So he turned back to go on his way.

"Hey, sport; how goes it?"

Someone was in front of him now, not three feet away. "What are *you* doing here?" he demanded.

"Y'know, Brian, answering machines kick ass; and sometimes they kick you square in the same place, since you never really know who might be around when you call," Gillian continued, her confidence gaining momentum with each passing second.

"Where's William? He was—"

"He's resting at home. I'll cut to the chase; you seem to have an issue with me. Please check that at the door. I'm a regular girl who only wants what's best for Will. He's been through hell and a half. We both, I suspect, want the same thing—for a friend to heal and be happy."

"You could start by coming clean and telling me who you *really* are," Vincent fired back. "Did you think when you hesitated so obviously to try and come up with an answer to Amy's question about your parents' death that somebody wouldn't raise a red flag? There were no records of any car accidents involving anyone named Moore in Manitoba province in the past 6 years. No deaths of any kind involving anyone by the name of Moore. So in your case, "Moore" is turning out to be less for you, and getting lesser all the time, credibility-wise."

"Fortunately, I don't have to answer to you; I only answer to Will, and I swear to God I only want what's best for him."

"You don't know what he's been through; he got stood up at the altar less than 2 months ago—"

"I *do* know; he told me tonight. Nasty stuff. He opened up to me about it. It was awful. I can't imagine the pain he's going through still. That's why there's no need to keep this investigation of yours going. For his sake, drop it. My intentions are on the up and up."

"You telling me to walk away? A woman who I don't even know, a woman who didn't exist, apparently until 5 weeks ago, telling me to stop digging around? What are you hiding, Gillian? I'm a reporter. So you can come clean now, or be outed later. Your choice."

Vincent threw down the gauntlet; this was deteriorating faster than a Daytona 500 race. If he was trying to scare her into telling him what her deal was, she surely didn't show it.

"You threatening me, Brian? Don't go down that path, because if you do, so help me God, you're in for a rude awakening. And that's not a threat."

He was dumbfounded Gillian would make such a statement, but before he could respond, he heard something else.

"Remember, Brian; I *will* protect him."

Coming from behind him, and sounding exactly like Gillian; he whirled around to see . . . no one. He turned back to confront her—

Only to discover she wasn't there. Anywhere. She couldn't have run away that fast, he surmised. No frigging way. No one else was within 50 feet. He did know two things, however. She was living with him and therefore, he needed to cool his jets until Monday, when he could take this to his attention without any interference from Gillian. Second, Vincent knew he couldn't take this incident to the police, because they can't act on mere threats. He left the park and went home, now aware of a third thing.

This just got a whole lot scarier.

Maybe he was way too confrontational with her, Vincent thought. He did pile on a lot, in hindsight. There hadn't been any semblance of a hint of trouble beforehand, and he felt afterward he took a ball bat to a hornet's nest. Those feelings were counterbalanced by a sense of duty he felt to his friend. All they had to go on was her word, and then that fateful moment when Amy asked an innocent question and it appeared Gillian didn't have an answer for a legitimate question. Once that gate is left open, doubts about everything else one says thus is fair game.

He parked his car in the driveway of their home and then gets out. He takes two steps toward the door when he walks into something; it seems like a wall, but he can't see it. He tries again to get into his house, but again, something holds him back.

Now he sees what is happening. A bubble is forming around him; like a bubble when the water is running into an empty glass, only much bigger and apparently impervious to any attempt to escape. Slowly the bubble is causing a damaging side effect; it's getting harder and harder to breathe. Vincent is suffocating, with no one around, no time to yell for help, and no breath to draw from. He is on the verge of passing out; no, dying. He slowly yields to the enormous pressure and falls to his knees.

Unaware, that is, of a second figure who seems to be standing outside of the bubble. Someone with a hairpin. In his deteriorated state, he can't make out who it is. But he recognizes the voice.

"I hold your mind in my hands. Think before you act, Brian. For his sake—and yours." The bubble then bursts . . .

The next thing he knows, he's awake in his bed. Alive. Breathing. And the clock showed 2:30 AM.

It was just a dream. That's all it was. His wife was sleeping soundly beside him, and was unawares of his labored attempts to catch his breath. That dream was too real, he thought. Far too real for comfort. It terrified him so. Brian tried for the next hour to go back to sleep but to no avail. Finally, sheer exhaustion took over and he fell off.

At that very moment, while Ross was sound asleep, a smile crept onto Gillian's slender, elegant face, lying beside him.

Message sent—and received.

Chapter 17

It was a peaceful night's sleep for William, considering his past 8 hours or so. It was 9:40 AM Sunday when he woke up and quite a sight greeted his return to the world.

"Morning, sleepy-head," Gillian purred, looking sleek in a blue tank top and cutoff jeans. "You seem a lot better, emotion-wise now than you were last night."

"I am. I hadn't told anybody what I was feeling; it took a lot out of me, but at least I got it out into the open. If I didn't tell someone how I felt, and soon—"

"The important thing is that you did, Will. And you're better off for it; you're a stronger person inside," she gave him a good morning kiss that rung his bell, among other things, and got up from the bed.

"Gillian, there's something else—"

"Me first, OK?" He had to know; no sense keeping it from him. "I pinch-hit for you last night. I went to see Brian while you were asleep. Needless to say, he was surprised beyond words that I showed up. We had a frank exchange of views, and in the end, I straightened him out," Gillian smiled coyly at this point, "and convinced him to end any further prying into something that really isn't his business to begin with."

He nodded his head in approval. "Cool—"

That was easy; I screwed around with this guy Vincent's dreams, and intimidated him into silence, and not a token amount of 'why did you do that?' from his best friend, Gillian mused.

"He means well, G; don't be too hard on him," Ross got up from the bed himself and offered her his hand. "Walk with me?" She did just that and they left the bedroom on the way to the main area of his apartment.

"You said there was something else?"

"Yeah; I was so off the charts upset last night that I meant to tell you this then, but need to clear it up now."

She suddenly tensed up inside. Now the heck what? Still keeping secrets? I'm from his own mind; I should know this stuff already.

"Two days after Sarah did what she did, the dreams began. The dreams in which you were front and center."

Gillian stopped cold in mid-stride. "What?"

"I was an emotional zombie after we left the church. I wanted no part of the real world, so I curled up into my own little self-made corner of it. Exactly like you see here, and on the outside; only minus the suffering and pain I was feeling, and that I would have a girl after all. I couldn't see her the first night after the wedding that wasn't, but the following night, I saw a face that matched my fantasy—your face, Gillian.

"Maybe some good did come from that ocean of heartache after all. You came into my life. And you're as alive, as real, as feeling for others as any normal person would. You know the best part, though?"

"What's that, sweetie?" Gillian wrapped her arms around him, now in the living room.

"You're all mine, if I may be so bold."

"Hmmm; you've got a pair on you, Will, I like that honesty. And I'm yours. Exclusively, totally, devotedly yours, where in this case, share and share alike doesn't apply."

Across town, a half-hour later.

The scene was starkly different in the home of one Brian Vincent. His sleep was a lot harder to come by. After all, he was at ground zero of a nightmare so terrifyingly real that it figuratively took his breath away—perhaps literally as well, and it was Gillian who was behind it. He got up at 10 AM and had breakfast with his wife Shondra and their three-year-old son, Naseem.

"So you going to tell William tomorrow of what went down, right?" she asked innocently.

"Huh?" He seemed a bit distracted to her, for whatever reason.

"Silly; you told me before we went to bed that Gillian threatened you last night if you kept checking her out."

Vincent's stomach was churning at this revelation. He forgot that he spilled his guts to Shondra last night. He had to do something to quell that. Now.

"I slept on it and decided I was wrong, honey; I pushed way too far and I'm not going to pursue it further."

She noticed his disturbed expression. "Is something wrong, Brian? You don't seem yourself this morning. Is there something you're not telling me?"

"No, it's just that I decided to change my mind," Vincent responded with a hint of sharpness in his voice. "I'm not going in that direction. It's not worth the time—"

"But what if she's leading a double life, or she's some crazy-ass lady who's—"

"Shondra, the matter is dropped. I came on like the Gestapo toward her; it was my fault. End of story."

She didn't want to provoke a petty argument over something like that, so she let Brian have the last word and finished breakfast without further incident.

He apologized for his testiness before Brian kissed his wife goodbye to head for the supermarket for the week's groceries. Shondra understood and waved him goodbye. A moment later, she picked up the phone and called someone, hoping against hope the one on the other end hadn't departed, too.

"Hello."

"Hi, is Rebecca there?"

"Sure is; can I ask who's calling?"

"Shondra Vincent, Brian's wife and his colleague at CityLife."

"Hey there; it's Kevin, her hubby. I'll get her post-haste."

A few seconds pass before a welcome voice greets Mrs. Vincent. "Shondra, hi; haven't heard from you in a while? What's the what?"

"At the risk of putting myself in the doghouse with Brian, I need to tell you something stranger than shit is going on."

"What do you mean?" Holm asked.

"Brian went to Balboa Park last night; he left a phone message for William Ross to meet him there, only he never showed. It turns out Gillian was there; she must've heard the message or Ross passed it onto her. There's no record of her, 'Becca. None. Brian wanted her to come clean, and instead was threatened by Gillian that he'd be in for a 'rude awakening' if he pursued it further."

"Shit . . ." Rebecca was in shock. "This actually happened?"

"Yes. This morning, though, Brian acts all weird and says he's dropping it. Something else happened to him, maybe, and he's not letting me in on it. We're OK and all; but I'm worried that she got to him somehow, and I'll be damned if I know how."

"It's good you called me. I've had the same doubts about her. My research will be a bit more discreet. Unfortunately, we can't go to the cops, not yet. But it appears Gillian's showing her true color."

"He said he might have been at fault for being too aggressive in his questions. Maybe Gillian just panicked and overreacted. Just being territorial, perhaps; it wouldn't be the first time a woman got defensive that way.

"Be that as it may, something's screwy, still. It's just he's been through the meat grinder with getting stood up, and we don't want him to get screwed again," Holm assured Shondra. "But I'll do some more checking; I've got some favors I can call in, maybe it will give us a clearer picture of who she is."

"Thanks. I gotta go, then; see ya." She hung up, knowing that someone else would pick up the slack.

Chapter 18

Ross's demeanor and outlook changed when he got into work that week. He was energetic and gung-ho, but there seemed to be a slight disconnect between him and his co-workers. It was little things at first.

William kept the paper humming, but he began to spend an hour or so every other day away from the office, telling everyone he was trying to round up new advertisers, but instead meeting Gillian back home for the proverbial quickie. He tried to be discreet about it, and quite frankly, he didn't care too much; his desire to be with Gillian was slowly overpowering his desire to put in a full day's work at CityLife.

After two weeks or so, he toned down the extracurricular stuff, and resorted to keeping his main office door closed for a an hour or two at a time, spending time on the phone with her, at the expense of a few advertisers and potential clients not getting phone calls back, and Ross getting a bit defensive whenever someone interrupted him with a story pitch or a phone call. The staff knew something was up eventually. His job performance was starting to take a bit of a hit, and the road he was traveling would not end at a happy place.

The kicker for them came one day when the work day ended, and Ross bid his co-workers goodbye as he walked home, only he seemed to leave something critical behind. He saw only blue skies and clear weather. The reality was quite different.

The city was being pounded with a rare rainstorm, and he left his umbrella at work. The five people who he trusted the most stared in sad astonishment. He seemed totally oblivious to getting soaked to the skin as he walked home as if the rain didn't affect him at all.

"Anyone for an intervention?" Amy Lloyd volunteered.

"Aye to that," Dan McCall said, and there wasn't a scintilla of doubt he spoke for the rest of them.

Later that night, the five are at a local watering hole a block away from the CityLife offices.

"We've got a problem," Amy being Ms. States-the-Obvious.

"As much as it pains me to say it," Greene began, "Yes. He's slipping into his own little world, which has only a passing resemblance to the one we populate. I do know his job performance is suffering, and Gillian is turning out to be an unhealthy influence in his life. She's all he ever talks about, thinks about. He still talks to us and all, but . . . I don't think we even register with him of late. Damn Sarah for leaving him at the altar like that."

"You blame her, Barry?" Rebecca wondered as she took a sip of wine. "It's not the first time a person has stumbled from one relationship to another."

"Let's think this through, people," McCall aimed to be the voice of reason, and could call himself a close friend of Will. "Yes, something's up. We all know that. Here's the thing; we need to tread lightly here. If he even smells a forced-upon intervention, it may drive a further wedge between him and us. We all care about William. None of us want to see him ruined, and perhaps now beyond repair, for a second time in less than 4 months. We've got to be discreet and understanding about it."

Rebecca took the point. "We have our jobs to consider, too. If he keeps down this path, the unreturned phone calls and what not, he may be fired, and us with him."

That created a uneasy silence over the group. Holm was right. It could have a ripple effect on the rest of the paper's employees. One among them was silent, listening to the ebb and flow.

"You've been pretty mute, Brian."

"Yeah, Amy; he does need our help. I've said from the get-go I don't trust Gillian. 'Becca, you've been with me on this opinion, right?" She nodded. "What we need to do is to figure out how to ease him into seeing what's happening—to bring him back to reality."

Just then, someone happened upon the meeting; a familiar face.

"Hope I'm not interrupting anything," the cheerfulness broke the gloom that pervaded the table. It was a friend from their past; now 29, unaware of the seismic changes that have taken shape where she once worked.

"Alison Kendall, as I live and breathe," McCall is dumbfounded and welcomes her to the group. Red-haired, blue-eyed and slender, she makes herself at home. "You know the gang, right?"

"Yes, it's been what, two years? Ever since the Union-Trib coaxed me to cover the computer technology beat."

"What brings you back to the big city?" Amy asked her. "And how did you know we were here?"

"I'm on vacation for a couple weeks. Your place of business hadn't changed addresses, and I told the security guard I used to work for the paper. I used to come in here after hours, so I figured this place would still be in your good graces, so I took a chance. I wasn't expecting you here; I'm lucky to burn, I guess." She took all the familiar sights in; her former co-workers, the jukebox at the far end of the bar, the ambiance. "It's good to be back home from being up north; the job pays a sweet amount of dough, but I do miss it here. Is William Ross still around?"

That stopped the conversation cold.

"Yeah," Greene said tentatively. "He's been through some rough spots of late, but he's still our editor and still kickin' it."

"I heard about the promotion. Also that he's off the market. Got married, or was about to, if memory serves," Alison suggested, not quite sure about the date of the wedding.

"Alison; it didn't happen." Brian said matter-of-factly.

"What?"

"She left him at the absolute last possible moment."

The revelation shocked Alison to her very core. "Jesus; I don't know what to say. I was crushing on him something fierce when I was here. Didn't dare let him—or you guys—see it. I never got the chance to tell him how I really felt."

An orgasmic rush silently came over Ross' friends. Their prayers had been answered. The solution had come from out of the blue, down from the north, and into a golden opportunity to save their closest friend.

"Alison—do you believe in second chances?" Barry Greene spoke for the quintet.

"Yeah. I do, actually."

"That makes five of us . . ."

And an idea is born.

Chapter 19

William and Gillian's love deepened, if that was possible, that weekend. Every second, every minute of his waking life was consumed by thoughts of her. They reveled in each other's presence, eating out on the town, jet skiing on San Diego Bay and dancing and loving the night away.

"C'mon, Will; bag Monday and we can spend more time together," Gillian lobbied him as they were in bed on Sunday night. "We've earned it. What's one more day?"

"Sorry, G, but Monday is the monthly staff meeting, which doubles this time as a road map for the last three months of the year, goal and production-wise. I've been slacking off a bit in that area; you wouldn't want an unemployed lover in a job market which is contracting more than you can say 'Montreal Expos' now, would you?"

Gillian sighed. "Yeah, you've got a point. So let's make this time even more memorable than every day before it."

"We've had some pretty off the charts days since you graced my world."

"Graced is one thing. Out and out rocking one's world is another." Gillian pulls the covers over both of them and they—let's just say, commiserate some more.

At the end of Monday's work day, a day marked by no shenanigans by Ross of any kind, he prepares to leave . . .

"See you tomorrow, guys-"

"Hold on there, Will; this day isn't officially over yet."

"What gives, Barry?"

"Spur of the moment thing; Buffalo Joe's is our next stop, and it's on us."

"Really? I'd like to, but I've gotta get home; Gillian—"

"She'll understand—it's not like we're gonna get you drunk and stuff," Rebecca assured him while keeping him inside the office for the time being by blocking the door, "And we'll have you home by 9, promise," she joked.

He thought it over. Will knew he spends a boatload of time with her. A few hours with his other friends wouldn't hurt.

"OK, then. That this is on your collective dime played a decisive part in me coming along." He wasn't afraid to whip out a timely quip of his own. "Lead the way."

Buffalo Joe's, about 20 minutes into their happy hour . . .

"You seem like you've been on edge the past few weeks," Dan began very cautiously. "We thought you could use some down time to unwind and kick back with us; if there's anything you need to unload on us, or one of us, we're here. You know that, Will."

"I know . . . I haven't exactly been the model of boss-dom lately. Things are getting tres' serious between me and Gillian, and I guess I'm letting that interfere with my work. Yes, interfere. She wanted me to play hooky today, but I put my foot down and said no, I couldn't. Otherwise, I'd have probably been on the receiving end of a well-intentioned intervention.

"I am happy, guys; Sarah is in the rear view mirror, at last. I've got a girl again, and hopefully five people who I'd walk through fire for."

The revelation caught everyone by surprise. There's no way he could have known about that, Rebecca said to herself. Amy picked up the slack, however.

"Will, at least you came in today. It was as if you've been in your own little world."

"I was in such a dank place after the non-wedding day, yeah. But be happy for me, OK? I've turned the—"

"Hang on; is that—"

"What, Brian?"

"It is; Alison!"

She noticed Dan waving his arms to signify where they were, and to come on over to their table was. "Hi, guys; long time no see!"

Ross didn't see who it was since he was sitting behind where she was coming from.

"Alison Kendall, what the heck you doin' here? How's the technology beat writer for the Union-Trib doing?"

"Just great, Amy. I've been on it for two years."

"Alison, I'd like to introduce you to William Ross, our editor." He got up to finally look at the former CityLife employee—and he was stunned. She was spectacular. Dressed in a pink blouse and skirt; and she worked for me?, he wondered. How could have he overlooked her?

"I do remember you, Miss Kendall. You were the entertainment reporter for us when I was assistant editor. You got the U-T job just as I got promoted to editor. We lost a good writer, and the Trib gained one."

"It's good to finally have a chance to see you and the gang informally."

"Would you mind joining us, Alison?"

"Whoa, 'Becca, this is Will's night out; let him make the call," Barry reminded her.

But there was no need for a recount of this vote. He had hardly talked with her when she was with the paper. Her beauty rivaled Gillian's if that was humanly possible. He offered her his seat, which she gladly accepted, and got another one.

Chapter 20

"How are things in San Jose, Alison?" William asked as the drinks were served as they bode time for the waitress to take their orders.

"Pretty good, Will. I do feel bad leaving you and the guys. It wasn't anything personal. Computers and how they tick have been for a while my second love. When the Union-Tribune had an opening for its tech columnist, for someone who's been immersed in what I've enjoyed half my life, I couldn't pass it up."

"You still call SD home?" McCall asked the returning columnist.

"I've got a place here, yeah; an apartment near the SDSU campus. The car gets quite a workout, though. Wish they had frequent driver miles on top of what I get at the Trib. It's discrimination, I tell ya."

They all had a good laugh at that. "Have you been OK? You went through a rough patch last year," Amy said with tenderness.

"Me and dad are tight; we leaned on each other after mom died. I'm glad all of you came to the funeral . . ." her voice trailed off.

"If it's any comfort, you turned out exceptionally well—there was no hesitation in giving you a recommendation for the U-T job. You earned that much. Your talent and ability shone through from the first day you were hired. I believe your mom would be most proud of how her daughter turned out."

Alison's eyes welled with tears, caught off-guard by his words. "That means more to me than you know, coming from you. You need to know that, Will."

There was something she felt for him; it took him that long to realize it, but now he knew. It only added to his confusion over who he cherished more; he had been blind to it, Alison's feelings for him. And what about Gillian, at home, wondering where he may be, since he didn't call ahead—and him not being particularly too distraught over that.

For the next hour and 45 minutes, they shot the breeze catching up on the past two years—including Sarah. Eventually, each of the crew had to depart to get some rest for tomorrow morning, calling it an early night. By the time 9PM rolled around, only Dan remained while William and Alison continued to chat.

"It's been a lot of fun reminiscing, Alison, but the missus beckons me home. I hope you enjoy your vacation here. See 'ya tomorrow, Will."

"You bet." Ross shook his hand and then there were only two. Alone, in a wall-to-wall crowded nightclub.

"So . . ."

"So; one more time that guy who said 'time flies when you're having fun was right. You seem like a quality guy, William. That's as common in this day and age as Anna Kournikova winning a women's tennis grand slam final. Hell, that's as common as her in any women's tennis final."

"Not that rare, Alison, please," he said in mock astonishment, grinning broadly and they shared a tender laugh. Now was her chance to tell him what she could not find the strength to do beforehand.

"Will—I never said this in the time we worked together back then, but I did have a heavyweight crush on you. I never let on; I don't know why I didn't. But seeing you again makes me believe in 'la energia del sino.'"

"La what?"

"'The power of fate.' I'm glad I met you; I never acted on it; dummy me. Are you—"

"I'm seeing someone, yes."

Her face fell. Damn.

"But I've learned something from tonight. Changing one's mind isn't just a woman's prerogative."

Was that a signal?, she questioned herself. Is he opening a door? Surely he wouldn't have said that unless something troubled him about his current status. She felt she had come to the proverbial fork in the road.

"How long are you here in SD, Alison?"

"Two weeks."

"Good," he said without thinking, without realizing it. He couldn't stop looking at her. Someone not from his imagination; but real, with an identity, an actual past. It made him feel normal again. "You said of a second love, but you never told anyone here your first love. What's that?"

"Not what, William. Not what." Alison took his hands in hers. He made no attempt to withdraw them. They were the hands of a woman who cared about him more than he could know. A fact he had not known until now.

Unbeknownst to either of them, one of his friends had hung around, and had for the past hour or so, eagerly viewing the evening's proceedings from a discreet distance, with a decidedly different opinion.

One of slow-boiling anger on her face.

Chapter 21

William came home 15 minutes later, at 9:10PM. What he saw when he opened the door to his apartment made him stop dead in his tracks.

Gillian was waiting for him, in a blue, slit to the thigh dress, like the one he bought for her at Victoria's Secret. She was an eye-popping sight. Her demeanor would be equally as revealing.

"Will; nice to have you home. How did the happy hour—or maybe I should say hours—go?"

"What?"

"And whoever she was who just happened to join you guys—very convenient of them—"

"Hold on; you were there?"

"You didn't even notice me. But you sure noticed her."

He was so caught up in the good time he had that he tuned everything and everyone else other than them out. "Look, I'm sorry I didn't call, but how did you know I was there? I didn't know I had to be at your beck and call."

"What I'm more ticked off at is that you fell right into their trap." Gillian hissed.

"Trap? What trap?"

"I thought you'd be smarter than that, Will—that whole dinner was staged. Nice touch to have their hand-picked home wrecker drop by during it instead of being totally obvious . . . real slick."

"G, she used to work for the paper. She's on vacation. There was no ulterior motive-" he tried to reason with her; she never showed this side of her before.

"You're getting played like a guitar, honey. Don't you see what's happening? They want to break us up. They told that woman to act like she was interested in you. They hate my guts enough to try this horseshit—"

"You're bonkers. I ask you again; how did you know where I was going to have dinner?"

"I'm a part of you, Will. You created me. We have a connection, you and I. I'm not sure what was worse; your quintet of so-called friends orchestrating this charade, or to see you actually interested in that bitch."

That remark was like a gunshot to the head. Now it was his turn to be hopping mad.

"You were spying on me? What gives you the right? I was being courteous toward her, that's all. There's nothing there, Gillian. There isn't even smoke, let alone fire."

That seemed to comfort her; somewhat. She turned a bit more docile in her tone. "They're eight ways from Sunday raging jealous of you, Will. They envy you in the company of a woman who's every bit their equal." She moved closer to him, her perfume just the right shade of overpowering and sensual. "And they'll do anything, even arrange a blind date to keep you from being happy. Nice friends, huh?"

Her hypnotic charm was wearing Ross down. He paused as her words sunk in.

"Will, I love you body and soul. No woman can—or ever will—come close to that. Don't let them tell you who to meet—or who to love. So take your stuff off, stay awhile, and give me some sugar." Gillian impulsively kissed him more passionately than at any time he had known her, in his dreams and otherwise.

Which led to more of the same . . .

Chapter 22

Barry Greene spent his lunch hour the next day in an outdoor cafe' not too far from the CityLife office on another cloudless, spectacular mid-day blue sky. He was savoring the prior night's events in his mind's eye. Sometimes luck *is* when preparation (the planned intervention) meets opportunity (the unexpected return of Alison Kendall). Maybe this will jolt Ross out of his stupor and bring him back to reality, he idly thought as he was finishing his lunch.

"Then again, maybe not."

He felt a hand on his shoulder behind him, and fear embraced his soul. Then, paralysis.

"No, really; don't get up on my account. And now, you can't. You can't move a muscle, Barry. I just thought it'd be nice to join you to celebrate your accomplishment." the visitor sat across from his table. He couldn't move one inch. His arms and legs were immobile, as if he was in a flight simulator pulling 5g's pinning him down. How?

"So, you were on hand last night, Gillian. If that is your real name, of course. Like what you saw?"

"Whoa; for someone whose mind I could really screw around with you've got quite a mouth. Needless to say," Gillian finished eating a hot dog as she flashed a smile his way. "Real, true slickness on your collective parts. But I'm here to tell you your matchmaking services will no longer be required. You see, Will's already spoken for. He's perfectly happy with who he has, someone who loves and cares about him. Now why do you and your posse have to go around mucking that up?"

"Because it's now profoundly obvious that you are not of this earth. What are you, and what do you want with William?"

"His love, and nothing more. Sarah almost destroyed him, Barry. He drew upon his own mind to make up for that loss. And I am the result of it. He gave me life, man, and we love one another. I will not tolerate any interference from any of your precious little clique. Ask Brian. The look on his face will tell all."

"You are mad. And I will do everything in my power to expose you to William and show him the person you really are," Greene was defiant, even if he couldn't slug her or raise a fingernail in resistance.

"William is exposed to me every night, and he revels in it. And you'll do nothing of the sort, as this will be our little secret, Barry," she got up and brushed her hand against his left cheek. "For if you tell a soul about this meeting, you'll see me in your dreams. And that will be a dark place, indeed. William is mine and mine alone, and no one will be allowed into our little world." She lets out that unmistakable, gut-churning throaty laugh . . .

Greene is a heaping pile of sweat as he scrambled out of his chair, awakened from his nap by a day-mare. My God, that did happen. It was so real. It WAS real. He whirled around to find Gillian, but she was nowhere to be . . .

Across the street, there she was, blowing him a kiss. A bus went past his line of sight without stopping—

And she was gone. Vanished. What the living hell is going on here? Except for the fact Gillian is a dangerous, powerful threat; not just to Will, but to all of his friends.

The events of the past 12 hours weighed heavily on Ross' conscience as he came into work the next day, unknowing of Gillian's improbable visit with Greene and its dark implications if he decided to tell him what had happened. So while cleaning up some overdue business, he closed the door to his office and thus began a internal evaluation of all that's occurred since Gillian arrived in his life.

The part of him who loved Gillian to the bone went up first.

> *What is so wrong with this picture, Will? You suffered something no human being should have to go through; you were abandoned by a woman who you thought had loved you. Through an extraordinary chain of circumstances and luck, another emerged from the ashes of that—a woman who was everything you dreamed about, since she came from that same place. Your mind. And since Gillian emerged from the darkness, you've been bathed in blazing sunlight. Life is too damned short to look a gift horse in the mouth. Until she does you wrong, if she does you wrong, enjoy it.*

And then, the other half of the argument.

> *Listen to reason, William; look at where Gillian came. Straight from a Twilight Zone. This is no TV show or movie; this is real life. She's not of this world, as alluring, as sexy and loving as she is. She's not a human being. Your friends suspect something's amiss; Brian, that you know of. And why didn't Gillian defer to you to confront him about the phone message. More importantly, why hasn't he said a word about it since? Could she have gotten to him, somehow? And what, God forbid would happen if somebody else outside your inner circle ask questions about her? How can she ever, EVER, find work, or have children, or have any semblance of a normal life? You have someone else who you didn't even know existed and now because of 'la energia del sino,' she's genuinely interested in you. So what if they set you up? They care about you, Will. More than you seem to care about yourself. Self-image has always been an issue with you . . .*

Just then, the phone rang. "Hello, William Ross."

"Will, hi; it's Alison."

"Alison . . . I didn't thank you enough for staying to talk after everyone left."

"You already did; you treated me with kindness, even though

I suspect you know your co-workers did arrange for me to meet you. I didn't seek them out, I swear—"

"It's OK; they mean well. It dawned on me later. But the night didn't turn out to be a bust."

"Listen, I was wondering, if you don't mind, maybe we could have—"

"Lunch?"

"Yeah. But you said you were involved with someone else."

He had to make a life-altering choice. What to do? Which side of his conscience to walk toward and embrace?

"Yes. But I'm feeling a bit unsure of where this is going. I've been living in my own little world of late. Is Thursday all right with you?"

"Definitely. The Prado at Balboa Park OK?"

"I've heard some good stuff about that. Deal, Alison. I look forward to seeing you then. Prepare to get your ear bent."

"That's what it's there for, among other things; take care, William."

"See 'ya then." He hung up the phone. It was only lunch, that's all it was. It wasn't a lifetime commitment, just an opportunity to see a former employee and talk. That's it. So why were his palms sweaty and his insides churning? Because he knew he had to keep it a secret from Gillian. How he would accomplish that would be another story indeed.

Since she came from the very place where he would have to store that secret and guard it as if his life depended on it.

Chapter 23

THURSDAY AFTERNOON . . .

If Gillian knew what was up, she wasn't letting on. He tried his best to maintain an even keel. He acted as if nothing out of the ordinary was going on. Same as in work, where he casually told his friends that he'd be taking an extended lunch today, which wasn't the way he operated when he had those afternoon liaisons with Gillian. When Amy asked in her usual direct way if the lunch was with Gillian, he simply shook his head 'no' and said he'd be back around 2PM. Perhaps it was the way he said it, but they seemed to believe him.

Barry Greene, however, called in sick today . . .

When he arrived at the Prado at 11.55 AM, he saw Alison already there, tastefully dressed in a blue top with a white skirt and elegant sandals to reflect the endless summer the city enjoyed. He had on a long-sleeve white shirt, khaki brown pants and brown shoes, which impressed his companion.

"You're lookin' sharp, William."

"You too, Alison," he tenderly shook her hand, being very easygoing, even if his insides were anything but. "Let's order some grub, OK?"

They both smiled as the waiter gave them menus in short order.

"I'm grateful you accepted my invite," Kendall began, measuring her words as much as Ross did his. "I wanted to explain in a little more detail my remark that I had a crush on you."

"And I'm glad I came, too. There's been some stuff in my life that's been bizarre and maybe if I talk it out with someone else, it'll be easier to deal with. So maybe we'll both find what we're after."

"That being?" Alison unexpectedly challenged him.

A pause. "Clarity. For things to be less murky and to be more out in the open."

"Yeah," she wasn't expecting that direct a reply. "It was all a matter of timing with me. About a year and a half ago, it dawned on me that you were a pretty cute guy."

Ross raised an eyebrow at that revelation. "I've been called many a thing in my day, but cute didn't happen to be one of 'em until now."

"I held that secret inside me for a while. I had no idea, of course, you were seeing Sarah, and when you announced your engagement that June day to us . . . it was like my heart had been put in a Cuisinart. It seriously bummed me out."

He knew the pain she described; he had gone through it before he met Sarah. "Alison, I'm sorry—"

"No sorrow necessary. Shit happens. I had built up a momentum of feeling sorry for myself until the Union-Trib came a-calling with a job offer that seemed too good to be true. The paper's main Silicon Valley writer relocated to Chicago and there was an opening that popped up. It paid better, to be truthful, and they liked my experience and my writing samples, so I wound up interviewing, and then getting the job. You had recommended me."

"I did. Bit my lip doing it, because I knew we were losing a very good writer, but the talent was there."

She continued. "Imagine my shock, then, when I stumbled onto your friends when I got back into town at Buffalo Joe's and they told me what happened. Not anything specific; just that it was over. Call me selfish, but I saw that as a second chance to tell you how I felt; and that it's Sarah's loss-"

"Alison, she left me at the altar."

That stunned her to her bones. It triggered something else—a tear in her eye. Several.

"God almighty, I didn't know, Will . . ."

"It was the catalyst for where I'm at now." Seizing the moment, now it was his turn. Her soul-cleansing had left him speechless for more than a few seconds. How could he have missed the signs that she had a serious thing for him? "I feel bad, because I didn't even notice. I was so focused on Sarah that I . . . that I concentrated on the life we were going to have. Then, she just done gone and left. It was as if a part of me died that day.

"Then someone else came into my life. She was everything my mind had crafted in a woman. It was as if," he had to be very careful at this point, "she came out of the blue, from my fantasy to rock-hard reality. Lately, I've been thinking about her every waking minute, and I mean literally, to the point where I've let my work ethic slack off, where I've shut out my other friends, and retreated into a reality where it's just her and nothing—or no one—else. I'm scared, Alison. She's like a living, breathing drug I can't get enough of."

It was an insight into a troubled mind that no one was allowed to see this close until now. It was a near-forgotten stranger to encourage him to open up. Alison drew in a sharp breath. "You love her; obviously. You're also scared of what the future holds. Which makes you no different from generations of men and women time immemorial who've had fear about the next step in a friendship. Isn't it better to recognize it now than later?"

"Yeah; I didn't think anyone could top Gillian—and then I saw you. I only looked at you as a quality employee. Never as someone more than that."

"So why start now, Will?"

Alison didn't answer him.

Out of nowhere, Gillian was but 10 feet away from the couple, decidedly un-amused.

"What are you doing here?" Ross demanded. "How did you know I—"

"Now now, darling, it all has to do with connections. And I believe you," she glared a 6-inch hole into Alison's forehead, "are making nice with my boyfriend."

"Look, Gillian, I don't know how you just popped up, but I have no desire to interfere—"

"Hold on, Alison, if anyone's interfering—"

"It's me? Is that it, Will?" Gillian finished what he was truly thinking.

"Will, I'd better leave before this gets even uglier than it is. I'm sorry. I'll see you around."

"Alison, please!" She hurriedly left the scene without saying another word. Now it was Ross's turn to be hopping mad. "You mind telling me what the hell that was about?"

"I can't leave you alone for a minute, can I?" Gillian seethed. "You're exhibiting a distressing habit of meeting people who want to break us up."

"You're in the wrong here, G; Alison is doing nothing of the sort. Our relationship has turned a dozen shades of weird. I have other friends who I trust and care about beside you. It's as if you want me to cut them all loose and spend all my time with you. How much is enough, Gillian? I do love you, but right now, I don't like you very much."

She would not back down. "First, you get snookered into that bogus happy hour when they spring her on you, then the very next week, you're having lunch with her. What am I supposed to take from that, Will? That you do feel something for her."

"It's like you're suffocating me, Gillian. I spend more and more time with you and it's never enough." Ross threw up his hands and began to walk away. "I've gotta get home; I need time to myself." He left her in very short order as he ran back to his car and drove off.

Ten minutes later, at 1:30PM, he was home. Ross needs some time to himself, that's all. Everywhere he's gone, she's been there to babysit him, almost. It was the redefinition of too much of a good thing. He needed to sort things out, to figure out where he would go from here. William pulled out his keys and unlocked the door to his apartment . . .

Only to find he wasn't alone.

Chapter 24

"You didn't think you'd get rid of me that easy, did you, Will?"

She was dressed in the same outfit when he first saw her in his dreams.

"How the hell did you get here? I sure as heck didn't give you a key, and public transportation isn't that efficient yet that you got here before me."

She smiled, then chuckled. "Do you think something as primitive as a key or a cab or bus can keep me from seeing you? You'll also see there's no forced entry, either. Like I said, we have a connection, the two of us. A bond stronger and more powerful than mere mortals will ever have. I can be anywhere you are in a heartbeat. I can do far more than enter someone's dreams; I can make them realer than real. There's a lot I can do that you haven't even seen yet.

"Thing is, Will, I love you. This world you call home, however, I don't love. At all. I'm here to offer you sanctuary in a place where there is no pain or despair. My world. Where you and I cherish and love one another, where time doesn't matter. Surely you don't think much of a world in which you've suffered so. I'm not Sarah— I'm your salvation."

Her words were weighing on his conscience by the moment; no matter. His mind was made up.

"As much as I love you, Gillian, your world isn't real. It's an escape. It's a cop out. It's where real people don't matter, where it's 24/7/365 of bliss. Real life isn't like that. I'd like it to be, but it isn't. I accept it. Why can't you?"

"Is that what you're made of? To settle for something less than what you really are? You created me, Will. Your imagination, your creativity, it doesn't know any boundaries. Why settle for something—or someone—less?"

"You keep saying I created you, like I'm better than everyone else; you've come across of late that you're better than anyone else—"

"Guess what, Will? We ARE better."

That stopped him cold.

"You heard me right; better. There's no one like me on this planet, and since you brought me into this world, there's no one on earth like you, either. We're special, and you need to embrace that. Love me, Will; leave your friends behind, and you won't regret it."

"I'm sorry, Gillian—you're not the only friend I have. I love you. But there are others I value as well. It can't be all you, all the time."

"Like you have a choice here."

Ross thought he misunderstood her. "Excuse me?"

"You heard me. I have nowhere else to go. And I don't intend to share you with anyone else."

That spooked him to no end. He turned toward the door and opened it. The door was opened, then he lost his grip on it and it slammed shut a moment later. He turned around to see Gillian smiling broadly.

"I guess the next thing you think I'm going to say is that 'if I can't have you, no one will.' That would be so passé, so Fatal Attraction-ish," Gillian said ominously, stepping back a couple of steps from William for an unknown reason. "The issue of whether or not we will be together and you being a part of my world is, rather, do you want to do it the easy way . . ."

His apartment ceased to be his apartment. There was a transformation into a blaze of black and red—and fire and smoke. It was as if he was instantly transported to hell itself. He was staggered to see what had transpired, and almost forgot that Gillian now had company on each side of her.

It looked like a pair of very pissed-off Doberman dogs, only their faces were shaped in a horrible, grotesque manner. Gillian was serene amid it all, keeping them in check by holding a leash on each of them.

"Or the non-easy way."

She dropped the leashes to the floor. He knew he would not be among the living if he didn't escape. Now. He prayed the door would work this time. If it opened, he had a chance.

It did.

The otherworldly dogs began their pursuit of him a second later as he slammed the door shut behind him. It bought him a precious few seconds, as he scrambled down a flight of steps and out the door. As he scrambled down, he heard a boom. He didn't turn back. As long as he kept running forward, as long as he was leaving the scene as soon as possible, he had a fighting chance.

Ross didn't know where he was going, but he did hear the unearthly sounds of his canine pursuers grow closer with each heartbeat. He couldn't run forever, and the dogs had no intent of slowing down. He didn't know what street he was on, only that he instinctively turned to his right to go down a block . . .

Where a bus was not 50 feet away from him and careening toward him.

No hesitation; Ross jumped out of the way of the oncoming bus and it barely worked. He did, however, hear a sickening thud. He knew it was against his better judgment, but he turned around after dusting himself off. Fortunately there were no broken bones.

Of the human kind.

Ross saw the bus driver get out and look at the front of the vehicle. Where two dogs lay bloodied and most assuredly dead, the front of the bus caved in as if a truck hit it. Out of reflex, he continued to sprint down the street, where a cab, without a passenger in the back seat, was coming in the same direction. He flagged it down and got in.

"Where to?" the driver asked.

"Away from here. I'll let you know in a minute, and there's a $10 tip if you be quick about it."

The cab sped away in short order. When the bus driver came back outside after he phoned in the accident, the scene was different.

As in lack of any dogs or whatever the hell they were. They simply weren't there anymore. Vanished without a trace.

Chapter 25

1:55PM.

"CityLife, Amy Lloyd here."

"Amy—thank God I reached you. I'm in deep shit."

"Will; oh my God . . ." she had to keep it together. "Guys, it's Will. He's in trouble." Everyone dropped what they were doing as she hit the speaker phone button.

"Get everyone together; meet me at Ruby's Mission Valley Diner ASAP. Things just went hellish, and quite literally, between Gillian and me. I've got to see you all. I need your help."

"What's your ETA, Will?" It was Greene talking.

"About 10 minutes. Hurry, guys, please. My life is in danger."

"We're outta here and we'll see you in minutes. Good luck." McCall said as he hung up the phone.

"There's something I've gotta tell you—" Greene said cautiously.

"Me, too," Vincent seconded that emotion.

"It'll keep. Let's get crackin.'" Rebecca snapped, the first one out of the CityLife offices, but not the last.

The diner, 8 minutes later.

Ross was already there, the fear on his face readily apparent. A few agonizing seconds followed as he looked around to find the five people he knew he could trust. "We're here, buddy." Brian Vincent spoke for all of them. Ross's spirits rose as quickly as tears came down his face. "Whatever it is, we'll deal together, man."

"Friends forever, Will. You know that." Rebecca Holm added with fervor. The six of them had a group hug, Ross's emotions in tatters right about now.

"I'm sorry, guys for all this. I haven't been straight with you, I've neglected my work, my friendships, everything, and I need to be honest NOW, before it's way too late. Gillian is more than she appears to be. Much, much more."

"Both of us," Greene said, motioning to Brian, "know where you speak. Now let's eat, drink and come clean."

He hadn't lost his sense of humor, that was for sure, William thought ruefully as they walked into the diner.

"On the Monday after the non-wedding, I had the most astonishingly vivid dream ever. It was real, even as it ended and I woke up. For the next month or so, the same woman dropped by every night as I was asleep, unabated, until the day in the laundromat. That was when Gillian emerged from a figment of my imagination—into the light of day."

The quintet were speechless. And more than a little disbelieving. But none of them dared interrupt Ross's train of thought. Not yet, anyway.

"When I came in that week with a spring in my step not courtesy of Viagra, you asked so many questions, and before I could say a word, you all wanted to meet her. I was between a rock, and a bigger rock. That's when, after Gillian agreed immediately that night to the dinner, a suitable bogus cover story was cooked up about where she came from. I didn't figure anyone would check it out. It almost worked, too, Amy, had you not asked her about how she wound up an orphan."

"I knew then something was amiss," Holm interrupted. "She hesitated a bit too long for comfort."

Vincent leaned forward to finally unload what he's been burdened with. "I started poking around the next day, discovering, eventually, there was no Gillian Moore of any kind. That's why I left the message on your phone, thinking you would come there to meet me. Only Gillian shows up instead, and threatened that I'd be in for a rude awakening if I pursued this any further. Which is exactly what happened later on that night."

"What are you talking about?" Ross's curiosity skyrocketed, knowing that it might not be what he wanted to hear.

"Will, that night, I had a nightmare; that I was trapped inside a big-ass bubble, suffocating; dying of lack of breath. I heard a voice that said they held my mind in her hands. Hers. Gillian."

"What?!!" said Ross, Holm and Lloyd nearly simultaneously.

"Gillian 'visited' me, too," Barry Greene piped up, now utterly and blissfully ignorant of the consequences she said would befall him. He had to know the whole story. "I was dozing off after I had lunch the day after we reintroduced Alison to you. She showed up, somehow, did something that I couldn't move an inch, and said if I breathed a word of it to anyone, she'd see me in my dreams. Well, screw her."

"*Screw her?* Such language, Barry; there are ladies present."

Everyone knew that voice. No one could do anything about it, however, for a wave of Gillian's hand kept them immobile—and mute. She pulled up a chair and sat in the aisle with them.

"Hail, hail, the gang's all here. You have no idea of the warm and fuzzies I'm feeling right now; a real Kodak moment, no?" She exuded complete, utter, total supremacy over them. "Now this is what I call a captive audience.

"A promise, up front. No one will be bodily harmed when I bring Mr. Ross here back into my arms. Emotional and mental harm—that's a whole 'nother ballgame. As much as I'd like to hang around and bond with the Super Six some more, I've got places to go. One place, actually. Tying up loose ends, yo? And Will," she got square in his face, "She won't know what hit her. It won't be on the level of luring my two pets in front of a bus like you did—props to you on that, however dangerous that was. But the wreckage I will inflict will be just as lurid. Bank on that."

Ross knew exactly what—and who—her next target was. Even if he couldn't move or speak, the abject terror in his face spoke for him.

"Then, at some point in the next 24 hours, we'll meet again. I know where and when. 'Cause it's not a matter of if, lover—but when." Gillian kissed him in front of everyone, a warm, sweet kiss from a cold-blooded being. "Ta-ta, all."

She leaves them and walks to the ladies' room of the diner not looking back. When the door closes, their paralysis and inability to talk ended. Ross, however, doesn't talk—he sprints to the restroom and goes inside.

But no one is there. He returns to their table, white as a sheet.

"Who's 'her', Will? I don't even know who . . ." now McCall did. "*Alison.*"

Group panic ensued.

"God almighty; does anyone have her phone number?" Amy Lloyd wailed.

Greene searched his mind for any clue, any speck of an exact location. "I don't even know her cell. She's in the line of fire and there's no way we can warn her or get to her. Do we even know where she lives near the SDSU campus?" His poise was crumbling with each passing moment, and it was a struggle to keep himself together.

Vincent offered this. "If she can enter people's dreams at will after they doze off . . . let's just hope she's awake. We can go back to the office—her last known address would be in her personnel file, right?"

"It's a reach—"

"It's all we've got. Maybe we can hit it lucky if she put her cell number in there, too," Greene said. "Will, what about calling the police and have them put out an APB?"

"Only thing is, how do we explain it—we're trying to find someone before they get whacked by a supernatural being?" Lloyd asked rhetorically.

"Do it. Let's roll." The six of them left the diner, heading back to CityLife on a wing and a prayer.

Chapter 26

A devastated Alison Kendall only now was just getting back to her apartment on the southwest side of the city. A half-week filled with such promise had gone to hell in a hand basket in record time. Will was gone, and a very nasty girlfriend who spooked her to her bones. Fortunately, she didn't have too much time left on her vacation, and she'd be back in San Jose before long.

She opened the door to her apartment; yes, the couch would be welcome for a dose of shut-eye.

The next thing she knew, an intruder pushed her to the floor. It was a man, but she couldn't see his face. His brute strength totally overwhelmed her as she tried to escape his clutches. Alison was losing the fight. She took a knife off the kitchen sink and tried to stab him, but he was much too quick for it. He knocked her down to the ground and then positioned himself on top of her so there was no means of escape. Alison screamed incessantly as the assailant began to tear apart her clothes layer by layer. She still couldn't see his face—she was being raped in her own apartment and she couldn't do a damn thing about it. Finally, Alison scratched at the faceless man and that seemed to reveal who he was.

William Ross's face.

She woke up screaming over and over again. He wasn't there. No one was there except her. The clock read 4:30PM. She must have fallen asleep and had the mother of all nightmares. A minute later, there was a pounding on the door. She scrambled toward the door, baseball bat at the ready. Alison opened it—

To see six people on the other side rush in.

"You OK, Alison?"

"No—I was . . . I thought I was being raped, and—" she saw William among them. "He raped me!" she backed away. "He was in here, and he punched and kicked and tore off my clothes—"

"No, Alison, he didn't! He's been with us the last hour and a half. Gillian did this to you; she screwed around with your mind but good," McCall assured her. William tried to move closer to her, but she freaked out.

"Get away, Will. You hear me?!" She grabbed a knife and held them at bay.

"Alison, it wasn't me. Gillian did this to you. Please; if you believe nothing else, believe that I would never hurt a woman in the way that bitch just did. She targeted you because you're a threat to her. Gillian is evil; she's the one who did this. I'm begging you, Alison; please believe me. I'm just glad you're alive."

"But how? It was so real. You were here, Will, not just 5 minutes ago . . ."

"No, he wasn't!" Greene snapped. "I know this is off the meter crazy, but you have to trust us. Please, for the love of God, Alison, trust him. You're going to be OK. Give me the knife, Alison; I'm begging you."

She gave William a good, hard look in his eyes for a half-minute, looking for any sign of treachery. Alison, however, found nothing but terror in his own face. He was deathly afraid of what happened to me, she thought.

They were not the eyes of a rapist.

She broke down and sobbed; and it was William who wound up hugging her tight. Gillian had tasted defeat—and it buoyed their spirits at a time when they needed a boost.

"C'mon; it's not safe here—we've got to get going. I'll explain as we go. We've got to look out for each other now." Holm said as they walked out of Alison's apartment. Even though they got to her in time, there was still no clue among them on how to deal with the evil in their midst. And what it would do to them if they allowed themselves to fall asleep.

The battle for Will's soul had not even begun.

Chapter 27

On the road, in Rebecca Holm's SUV van . . .

"How did you know where I was staying?"

"We didn't. When you happened on our get-together before we introduced you to William, neither you nor us thought of exchanging phone numbers. We didn't think anything of it. Fortunately, Dan found a way of locating you," Amy Lloyd said.

"I called up the Union-Trib, and called in a favor. They were most helpful in telling me where you were. Lord knows what would have happened if we stumbled around the city looking for you, not knowing what the hell Gillian would do to your mind."

"She's responsible for all this?"

"Yes," Ross replied, a bit withdrawn from the conversation. "Gillian came from within my mind. And it's obvious to even me that possessiveness has become her primary characteristic. She perceives all of you as a collective threat to her."

"She wants you all to herself, Will," Rebecca said, taking a moment from concentrating on the road in front of her. "How could you have let loose such a thing on the world?"

"She's not a 'thing', Rebecca. She's flesh and blood. You think I'm a mad scientist or something, or somebody who watched 'Weird Science' one time too many and created a girlfriend with my own hands? It was just circumstances beyond anyone's control. It was wonderful. Until now. And I don't have a clue as to how to deal with it."

"It's obvious; she needs to be dealt with. She has powers beyond what anyone can handle. The police—"

"I don't think I like where this conversation is going, Rebecca. You obviously feel threatened by Gillian as she is with all of you. What you're advocating is a permanent solution, if you get my drift."

"She's not human, Will. She's put us in danger, and you went along with her. You aided and abetted her in the beginning, and now this thing is out of control."

"Stop the car, right now!" Ross yelled. She did, and pulled it into an empty parking lot, where Ross got out, ready for verbal battle. "You have a problem, Rebecca? Let's hear it; we're all grown-ups here."

"You're the problem; you lied to us, Mr. Ross. We're your closest friends, and you could've come clean about this . . . person, but you didn't. You were goddamn selfish, you weren't thinking straight even after Sarah left town. You still haven't dealt with it. You put it on hold."

"And what would all of you have done if I told you then what I told you today? You'd book me in front of a shrink, or have me sent to Betty Ford. I didn't mean to lie; I was happy again. Damn you, I was due after getting f'd like that."

"If she was a normal person, I don't think any of us would have batted an eye. But she's not. She's . . . it's—"

"You're jealous."

The remark flattened Holm's combativeness. "What?"

"Gillian made mincemeat out of you at the dinner; even before Amy waylaid her, you were itching to discredit her—make her look like shit, and you didn't get the job done."

"Well, who's laughing now, Will?" Holm was almost nose-to-nose with her boss, not willing to retreat one millimeter.

"Enough!" Alison yelled. "Whatever Gillian is, we're not going to deal with her successfully if we're fighting between ourselves. What we need to do obviously is to stay awake, since she seems to thrive whenever we're asleep. Can we at least agree on that?"

Both Ross and Holm retracted their claws momentarily and nodded.

"The question now is, where do we go? We have to find a place to stay."

"Easier said, Brian," McCall intervened. "She can travel from one place to another as quickly as a Randy Johnson fastball. Is it going to matter where we wind up? Gillian said in 24 hours, she would be back. As long as we can stay awake, we can brainstorm and try to deal with her. So where do we crash?"

"My place."

Everyone looked most skeptically at William, but his facade was resolute.

"It may be the last place she'd look, especially since I was running like Jesse Owens to get away from it when she turned bad. And I want to be on my turf when the final battle happens. Home-field advantage always helps. Anyone who wants to bail now, you're welcome to. That said, ultimately, it's me she wants. This is my fight, and as bad as I feel right now for lying to you in the past, the thought of putting any one of you in harm's way even more than I already have, I can't ask that of you. It has to be your choice."

Even with nerves frayed beyond belief at this point, no one bolted. Friends to the end, Ross thought.

No matter what end was nigh.

They motored around for about another half-hour before they made the fateful trip back to Ross' home on 6th Avenue.

"Looks like there aren't any paranormal things around," quipped Alison

"As with trying to find someone to love, it's what's on the inside that counts," Ross took the point as the six cautiously walked into the building and up to his second floor apartment. He calmly took out his key, opened the door . . .

And found everything where it was supposed to be. Pristine, actually. "Just think, a few hours ago, this was a pretty good imitation of a hell dimension," Ross said. "We've got a long night ahead of us, so who wants pizza?"

"Pizza? How can you think of food at a time like this?"

"Easy answer; I'm not going to wait around and twiddle my thumbs until Gillian decides to make her grand re-entrance in here. We'll eat, we'll drink, and we'll talk. We need to talk, to clear the air, to come clean. To deal."

That last thing got their attention. "Of course, cheese steaks would be the primary choice, food-wise for me, but we're about 3000 miles away from the closest restaurant for that. So consider this a boss inviting his employees over for an all-nighter." Ross knew that lame attempt at humor would not go over too much, but it cracked the tension a little bit.

"Why not?" Barry Greene spoke for them all.

Now it would be a waiting game.

Chapter 28

So a few of the gang were chowing down on pizza while watching a movie on Will's DVD player. He and Brian, however, were in an intense game of video baseball on his console system.

"This will not be a 'two-out, bases-loaded, bottom of the ninth' end to this tale, I'm afraid," Vincent said, his Yankees holding a 5-1 lead on Ross's Seattle Mariners.

"I'm sure that's what the Giants were thinking in the 7th inning of game 6 at Anaheim, too," Ross joked as he went up to bat.

"This is my fault, of course."

"What's your fault, Brian?"

"I left that message on your box, naively thinking Gillian hadn't moved in with you. But now that I think it, where else could she go? That set everything in motion."

"If you hadn't, then none of us would have discovered Gillian's other side. Everyone has one; the trick is to keep it in a dark place, never to see the light of day; not to let it consume you. Gillian nearly consumed me, Brian. So good; everywhere."

"Everywhere?" Brian kind of knew what he was implying.

"Here, too. There, especially," he pointed to his bedroom.

"I hear 'ya, dude. Damn, struck you out with the vicious change up. Game over." He pats him on the back in a gesture of consolation. "You think Gillian can be reasoned with?"

"I wish I knew. The acrimony we have, as in me and her, plus how much of a threat she wrongly thinks you all are may be too much to overcome. But she came from me; so there's humanity in her, as there is in me, you, everyone of us. If that isn't extinguished totally, there's hope. I don't want this to be two enter, one leave. Neither of us, I suspect, will escape unscathed."

5 A.M. came and went, and after a spirited game of poker, they were all staring at the TV, watching an infomercial for some new cooking gadget. Ross was amazed.

"I used to get up sometimes when I was younger and all I saw on a TV this time of night was a test pattern. Now it's a haven for every wannabe entrepreneur hawking one thing or another. The ab-sizer; shake those pounds off; the rotating chicken-cooking thingies; it never ends. Give me a test pattern any day."

He sighed; the fun and games and food were winding down, and the reason why they were all in his abode and what led them to this moment came down on them.

"Will, you told us that you let Gillian in on what happened that day, the day when . . . when Sarah took a powder," Rebecca hesitated, but all in all simmered down from earlier on with her confrontation with him. "Right?"

"Yes. I spared her how I really felt, just told her the particulars as a writer would present the facts of a story. She had already been a healing influence beforehand. Being with her at the beginning made me forget about Sarah real fast. It accelerated putting that part of my life behind me."

"This is going to sound real intervention-esque, but you haven't confronted your own feelings about it. You only hinted at it, I guess, with Gillian," Brian continued. "But like a friend or family member dyin', you've got to reconcile your feelings with you. You can't keep it buried much longer."

Amy tried her luck once more. "All you've done is put it off, postponed dealing with it. You haven't moved on and until you do, it will eat at you like an ulcer, a cancer. We didn't hear from you for two days afterward. So we care about our boss. Sue us, then."

A very long pause. He said himself the time had come to deal. Time to back those words up.

"The weird thing is, I didn't have a drop to drink," Ross began. "I was home the whole time, shut off my answering machine, isolated myself. Drinking is supposed to numb you, a cheap-assed way to remove any pain you have. I was already at that point. It's as if I walked into that church full of life and hope, and every emotion I had was removed in there.

"I was in a daze. I don't know how I got home that day since it felt like I was sleepwalking through it. The worst part? There was no warning. I didn't see any signs that this was a doomed thing. I let myself get so wrapped up in the future, and what it would hold that I didn't realize that something inside me made Sarah major queasy about spending the rest of her life with me. I was the cause. Something in me made her walk away, and I don't know what it was. And I never will. Maybe I don't want to know.

"Saturday and Sunday I just was so out of it. I hadn't thought of suicide. Didn't have a chance to, in the end. I was staring at a few days off from CityLife when early that Monday morning, I had the best dream of my adult life. Even when I woke up from it, I knew I was living it. Gillian must've been someone I saw on TV, or pictured from other women in my past. Parts of them come together to create someone who Gillian wound up as. I've never hated anyone with any real feeling. But I hate Sarah," he felt himself losing his resistance to say what he truly felt. "I hate her. I hate myself. She ended my life, and Gillian brought me back from the brink." Ross began to cry at this point. "And at any moment, I'm going to have to face her, and you all wanting me to 'stop' her. I don't know if I can. I don't know if I want to. I want her in my life. I want her to accept you and have it done in return. But it can't. Damned if I do, damned if I don't."

There were no words they could convey to show how much he was loved. But their mission was accomplished; he told them how he felt, he dealt with his grief. He bonded with his friends, his friends who have histories and pasts. He excused himself and retired to his bedroom for a few minutes. No one moved a muscle. Each of them knew they couldn't comfort him—or prove him wrong. They did want her stopped, out of the way; they were more fearful of what they thought she was capable of doing, not what she had already done.

Each of them—except one . . .

Chapter 29

It was around 5:30 AM now, their all-nighter almost complete without anyone dozing off to Ross' surprise. They had survived. But there was a long road ahead, and they had to be in work in less than 4 hours.

He heard a knock on his door. "Come on in. If it's Gillian, then let's finish this here and now."

It was a woman, but not whom he thought it would be.

"You OK, Will?" Alison was in the doorway. His expression spoke for him. "That bad . . . would you like some company?"

He nodded. "I feel like shit right now. You know why? Because I finally let loose with my feelings about what happened, and Gillian, in front of someone who thought enough of me to confide she had feelings of her own toward me. I am so screwed up in the head right now. The waiting is the tortuous part. I don't know if I have the strength to resist her. I'm not sure if I want to turn my back on her. The last 2 months have been so right, so sweet. Why look a gift horse in the mouth?"

"Because you need to reacquaint yourself with reality. You retreated into a world where all is sweetness and light, and there's nothing wrong with that. As long as you do your grieving and get back in the game. But you haven't yet. You've languished in self-pity for far too long. You're better than that, William."

The harshness of Alison's rebuke took him aback. "Alison, I'm sorry I didn't realize that you felt something for me. I could use a friend right now."

"You have a friend in your midst. You have five more of them out there who are willing to stick their necks out for you. We care. I care. More than you can begin to comprehend." She leaned down and kissed him on the right cheek. "Some more than others." He turned several different shades of red as he looked down at the floor in slight embarrassment. When Ross turned to look back up at Alison . . .

Someone else was behind her.

"Your friends setting you up with him; seeing him for dinner, and now *kissing* him. That's as good a 'three strikes' rule as any."

Gillian wrapped her arms behind Alison and tossed her out onto the apartment's main area; she flew 15 feet before coming to a crashing halt against the television table. The rest of them scrambled to come to her aid when they saw Gillian back in their midst.

"I said I'd be back, folks. I may not be prompt, but I always keep my word. I'm going to borrow your boss here for the next few moments." She waved her hand—and they vanished. They were now alone in his apartment.

Chapter 30

"Where are my friends? What have you done with them?"

He didn't know if they were dead, alive, or in between. She was dressed in a conservative beige dress, pink skirt and elegant 2-inch-heeled shoes. Her hair was drawn back in a ponytail and makeup elaborated her round, sweet face with those smoldering lips. The antithesis of someone who has developed quite the mean streak.

"In a place where they can't help you. Not even to lend moral support. Just you and me, baby. The way it's been, and the way it will be again."

He suddenly lunged for her throat, but he missed her and fell on the floor. Only he didn't miss her; he ran through her, tripped and fell. Gillian laughed at her lover and offered him her hand to get up. Gillian somehow changed herself to be impervious to any physical assault on her person.

"File that under one of those things I can do that I didn't let you in on," she said, enjoying every moment of his new situation. "Nice touch, coming back to the place where I was born. Please do believe me when I say I really wasn't going to lay a finger on you. That would be so not productive for me, or you. Not to mention so very wrong."

"But you're willing to put others in danger, to screw with their dreams and make them think folks raped them, to get what you want, right?"

"Hate to burst that bubble, Will, but you're hardly the only aggrieved party here. We're drifting apart, and I'm merely taking steps that will ensure our love will remain intact."

Ross tried the nonchalant route, even if his insides were far from chalant. "Yeah, what-EV-er, you made your grand entrance, big whoop. Now do me a favor," he walked over to his front door, "Don't let this hit you in the backside on the way out, OK?" Ross opened it, only to discover a pitch-blackness in front of him, and below as well.

He was about to plunge downward into an endless abyss; nice time for a bout of vertigo before he regained his bearings 15 seconds or so later. The color was drained from his face as he turned to look at his enemy.

"What you failed to comprehend, until just now, I think, is that you're in MY yard, Will. You may think you have 'home field advantage' as you lamely put it. Instead you and your posse slam danced straight into my . . . OK, trap."

His stunned look spoke volumes, and Gillian seized on it.

"You thought that by pulling an all-nighter, you'd deny me the chance to return. So I simply bided my time until you were well and good sleep-deprived to make my move. Alison did rush the timetable a bit. It was so easy tossing her out of my way like a rag doll. So unworthy of you." A wicked smile followed.

Ross stepped toward Gillian with hate in his heart, but she stops him in his tracks when she held out her left hand. He couldn't move, but could speak. Maybe. She surveys her prey casually, as she is most definitely in control of the agenda.

"Here's how this is gonna go down, sweetie. This is my world you're in, and there's no escape from it. The same as yours, minus the distractions, the troubles—and the pain. If you, here and now, embrace this world as your own, your friends will be returned to their lives and it will all be over in a snap. They won't know who you are, of course. And we will love one another for however long you have left on this earth. No immortality deal, sorry; I don't have that much stroke with the cosmic forces that shape everything around us—and your significantly creative imagination—to broker that kind of good mojo. But it will be a world where love and happiness reign hand in hand; where we go through life hand in hand."

It was what he experienced from the instant she came into his life. He was happy. Sarah was nothing but a bad memory. He deserved to have good karma go his way. But Ross also knew that everything came with a price and that outweighed the good.

"Nice offer. Even though we're in California, I guess I won't get anywhere saying 'I'll have my people contact your people, no?'"

Gillian shook her head. "To the end, a sense of humor. I love that. I love you, Will. What's so bad about this?"

"Suppose—just suppose, I decide to turn my nose up at your offer? What then?"

Her mood swung in an instant. A beautiful face was replaced by silent, yet palpable rage. She had been turned down. To Gillian, it was the last straw, the final bridge which was about to get washed out by a flood.

It was still his apartment, so it didn't seem like anything had changed.

Except for the cane beside his bed.

This was three years ago. When he was about 35 percent heavier than he was now. Ross had let himself go far too much, and he was in the danger zone in just about every way, health-wise. His back had given out time and time again and he needed assistance just to get around. The pain that shot through his bones was not remotely close to the humiliation he felt when he had to go into the outside world and have people see how bad he had gone. He had never seen himself as others saw him. Until then. He had no words to come back at Gillian with. Not even the fact he knuckled down and got his act together. Being like that had cost him years of relationships; who knows how many. Ross looked a shamed, beaten man already, and the showdown was just beginning. He knew he had to steel himself better against her.

"Nothing like going for the knockout punch early, right? You see, Will; since I came from your mind, I'm privy to everything that's in it. Specifically, memories. Some forgotten, some remembered still, years afterward. A library of things that define who you are. Every one of them easily accessible by its current 'librarian'; me," Gillian pointed out as she loomed over Ross, on one knee, not looking at her.

"I can make you relive any event in your life that I see fit. A word of warning; each memory I dial up for you will be worse than the previous one. You and you alone have the power to make them stop. Just say that you love me and accept what I've offered you. That's all. Or we can go the long way around. So what'll it be, lover?"

He thought about it for a moment, then rose up to his feet, fists clenched in a discreet manner.

"Is that all you've got, G?"

The apartment dissolved into another scene, this time outdoors.

It was Balboa Park. He had no choice, no escape plan; she was running the show and no matter if he liked it or not, he was an unwilling witness to it. He could see himself with his eye on a girl on a park bench near the waterfront.

"For all your successes, William, in the getting-to-know-one way, there have been more than your share of misses. A lot more, including ones that cut to the bone . . ."

He knew when, now. This was in 2002, sometime in the fall. He saw himself walk over to her, almost there, only to see another girl enter the picture and get there first. She recognized her, got up—and kissed her.

"Too bad for you; that was but an extreme example of your many near-misses with women. I will admit, though, they look made for each other, no?"

Ross glared at Gillian with hate in his heart, but before he could put it in words, another scene followed; this time at a diner where he had his eye on a woman, but she eventually told him she was spoken for. Again, he knew exactly where and when. In the next 60 seconds, one misfire after another was laid out for him to see, helpless to stop the rewinding of the past Gillian laid out for him. All of it true, all of it hurtful. Each memory revisited of being rejected or not even getting a chance to make a good impression representing a twisting of the virtual knife.

The tapestry finally changed back to where it was. His apartment; her turf. Her rules.

"Is that all I've got? No," Gillian said as a little more of Ross's will to fight the war she waged on his psyche diminished. "What you've got in you to resist me is open to debate, however. You hurt me, Will. You gave me life, you gave me purpose; you gave me love. And now you want to discard me when I get too close. That's why you've never married. You've always kept your guard up. Denying people from seeing the good man you really are."

Ross was clearly drained by that encounter. It would get even worse from here; he was losing the will to challenge her. This was mind-rape that she was doing. Nothing else.

"You say you love me, but all you're doing is hurting me. I'm not perfect, Gillian. I'm no God, either, but if there's a speck of humanity in you, you'll see that this road will lead us both to ruin."

"No, just one of us. You're all I have, William, and I won't let you slip away to Alison. Not to any other woman. I ask you again; will you join me in my world?"

"In lawyer-speak, objection, your honor. Asked and answered."

"Damn you!" Gillian hissed at him, as mad as he had ever seen her. "Do you have a death wish? I guess I haven't tried hard enough. No matter. Weakness is a trait you've always had in the past. Especially . . . ."

The apartment disappeared again, replaced by a damning image; a few blocks from his childhood home. He was back in grade school where he was being chased by 6 classmates redefining what a cowardly bully posse is.

"Will he outrun them? I love chase scenes, don't you?" Gillian taunted him as he tried to close his eyes. Only she would have none of it. "Now now, Will, no dozing off or not paying attention!" She made it so that he could not close his eyes at all.

"And your point is what, exactly?"

"Don't you want to know how it ends? 'Sides, there'll be a quiz on this at the end of the presentation."

"So the hell what, G? I already know this stuff."

"This is to just reacquaint you with your inner wuss. Why didn't you fight back? Why let them have their way with you the way they did? Because you were afraid; you didn't want to rock the boat."

"Afraid? Afraid of killing one of them if I cut loose, yes. Guilty. So I turned the other cheek."

"Bullshit. You turned toward what you really are away from work. There, you've made the right moves, but away from it, you zigged when you should have zagged. You let people walk all over you and you put out the damn welcome mat. That's why you've drifted from relationship to relationship, that's why you looked the other way when your clueless clique set you up with Alison to spite me, and that's why you were actually giving her the time of day. You settle for less, Will; always have. It's like you don't think you're worthy. But you ARE worthy; you realized that when I came into the mix, and you damn well know it."

Ross was an emotional train wreck. The tears flowed unchecked down his face, he was on both knees, as if he took a beating which brought him to the ground. His fighting spirit was almost extinguished. He couldn't take one more flashback, especially since he may have an idea of what it would be.

"Gillian, please . . ."

"Please what, Will? Please *stop*? You know how to stop it. The thing is, you've done it before, countless times. Why do you have such a hangup about taking the right fork in the road? Do you actually think you can outlast me in this test of wills, do you? C'mon, Mr. Ross; tell me I don't stand a chance."

"I don't have to; you just did."

For the first time since their final showdown began, it was Gillian who was stunned into silence.

"And you're not the Gillian I loved. Rest assured, I will escort you off this world as quick as I brought you into it." He knew that this was his last stand. Ross willed every ounce of defiance he had left into drawing the line in the sand here and now.

"Umm . . . maybe news travels a bit slow around here, but at this particular moment, I've got you by the balls, and class is dismissed only when you renounce your deeply flawed world for one where there are no such flaws. Only goodness. Only love."

"Love? The Gillian I'm looking at doesn't know the meaning of the word. She's a user, a worthless, scheming—"

He couldn't move a muscle again as Gillian stalked toward him. "You good for shit son of a bitch!" She clocked him square on the jaw with a thunderous right cross, the pain of which was searing.

"Yeah, I'm feeling the love. Two syllables, Gillian; lo-ser."

She grabbed him by the throat and lifted him into the air, then a moment later dropped him back to terra firma. And smiled. "Nice try, slick-meister. Getting me mad enough at you so I'll dump you. When I came from you, I also retained your smarts. I'm much too smart for that."

The light bulb went on. That was it. If he had memories she could exploit, and how the natural order of things don't apply in her arena, then maybe two could play that game. He closed his eyes . . .

"Believe this, William; I've got one more walk down memory lane on tap, and it WILL break you. And once our reconciliation occurs after that, all your puny, insect, lame-assed friends will be in my sights, every last one of 'em. For after I get through with them, feasting on them while they sleep, they're gonna think Freddie Krueger is the Easter Bunny on the nightmare-creation food chain."

"Not on my watch, you won't."

Ross didn't answer her. That voice came from behind him, which meant Gillian saw it first. What he saw in her eyes was an emotion absent from the time she imprisoned him in his own home until now.

Naked, unrelenting panic.

Chapter 31

"Get away! You're not welcome here!" she shouted. William turned around to see what she was now so frightened of. The sight nearly made his eyes pop out.

A second Gillian.

Dressed differently, in a white blouse and black miniskirt, but it was surely her. A copy, but why? Was it a trick that would seal his fate or give it a new lease on life? Friend or foe?

"I wouldn't exactly call myself a *speck* of humanity, Will. Not Anna Nicole-esque, either; somewhere in between."

Ross' spirits skyrocketed; he had his answer.

"Gillian, it's good to have you back."

"She's lying! I'm Gillian; don't listen to that thing!"

"Why? Are you afraid of her? Are you afraid of the humanity that came part and parcel with Gillian?"

"You said it yourself, Will," the new participant in the fray said to Gillian, who was gripped with increasing nervousness, and he noticed it. "Every one of us has a dark side," subtly pointing her finger in Gillian's direction, "and unfortunately mine has been abusing her time on this earth like a drunken sailor. She's put you and your friends at unacceptable danger."

"What you don't realize, lady," Ross continued the assault on Gillian's dark half, "is when you were made flesh, you now have memories as well. Not as extensive as mine, but memories just the same."

"And I've one memory that's waiting for the right moment. Like now . . ."

A moment later, the scene switches to Buffalo Joe's, one he remembers. Gillian was at his side, still, along with the other Gillian. Without warning, he saw the woman he loved morph into Alison Kendall.

He was shaken to his bones at the transformation. Could she be pulling her ultimate trick on him?

"What you fear most, my dark alter ego, is this—" then, quickly, she whispered to William this:

"Play along if you want to get outta here."

She kissed him in front of his captor, milking the moment for all it was worth. It sounded like Alison, which made the moment even more realistic. Gillian could do a lot of things, Ross thought. If we get out of this, I'll thank her for it.

The moment devastated the other Gillian. She collapsed to her knees as if she'd been shot. That was her ultimate weakness. She was unveiled to be shallow, possessive and when she didn't get her own way, strikingly immature. She was losing this, and was becoming more desperate by the second.

"Will; please believe me. She's the one who has the agenda, not me," she began walking casually toward them and with rising purpose. "She's the one who needs to be put down-" she kicked Gillian in the stomach and sent her flying across the restaurant, which became his apartment again. "You can't stop me, William. You love me, not her, not Alison. Say it. Please."

"I don't love you!" he shouted.

For a minute she seemed to actually fade somewhat. It gave him an idea.

"Please, Will; love me; embrace my world. It's not that hard; I'm the Gillian who came from your mind—"

"Get out of my life! You disgust me; you hurt me, you put my friends in harm's way. Hardly the acts of someone who claims to love me."

Again, she seemed to emulate a TV show or movie when it faded to black. Every insult registered on Gillian like one body blow after another. Ross turned to see where Gillian was, which was 20 feet away. He ran over to her and cradled her head in his hands. "You see Gillian here? She's the one I love, not you."

"No!" she cried out, and then she did cry. "I beg you, Will; please don't kill me. You're killing me. You do it, and you'll never be with another woman. I will haunt you the rest of your life. I swear by all that's holy."

So that was her last stand; the guilt card. Ross hesitated. What if she was right? She certainly was capable of entering people's dreams at will and with impunity. Would he be lonely for the rest of his days? He turned around to face her, emboldened with resolve.

"Better to be real than to live in fantasy. I'm so sorry; God forgive me. I don't love you."

She didn't utter a word. The tears flowed unchecked down her cheeks—and his. She withered away, vanishing into the air. She mouthed, "I love you, William" as she departed his apartment, his life, and his world. He gently laid Gillian's head down on a pillow and sat down on the floor of the living room looking longingly at her.

Ross noticed nothing had changed, though. Since the other Gillian was defeated, his friends should have been returned to him, but they weren't.

"They're OK."

He turned around and saw Gillian—the real one—standing behind him. She was OK. He no longer could help himself. He kissed her time and again, she returning the favor. "God, I knew you had a sense of right and wrong, that there's good in you. You came from me, G; and I'm thankful that you saved me. And my friends."

"William—"

"Now that your dark side is gone, we can make plans for the future. Our future. We can make it work, Gillian; I love you far too much to abandon you. I'm just glad you're back."

"I'm sorry my worse half got the better of me. You saw me at my best—and worst. It's a package deal. Which means in a few moments, I'll be joining her—as part of your past."

He knew only then what she meant. It hit him like a knife wound.

"No . . . I can't; I can't bear the thought of a life without you.

You rescued me from the depths of my despair, Gillian. You can't leave me now."

"It's *because* I love you so that I have to," Gillian held his hands with her own as she separated from him. "The creativity, the imagination, the love you have for others; it's wasted in my realm. Fantasy, as exhilarating as it is, is no match for reality. It shouldn't be. And it's time you got back in the game."

"Why, Gillian? Why leave?" He couldn't stop the tears; the thought of her leaving was beyond unbearable. "I need you."

"Because you need to start living again, Will. The time we had together I will always cherish. I had said how I didn't like your world very much. I was wrong. It's the only world you've got. You've got people who care about you. You have one who I believe loves you even more than I do. You need to live again. You've got to live every moment and cherish it. For as quick as that moment comes, it goes away. If you reside in my neck of the woods too much, the years will rush by, and there'll come a time where you will wonder where it all went. I don't want that fate to befall you.

"You gave me two months of utter, absolute joy. Two months that I never would have had if not for your mind's eye creating me. You are a God to me, sweetheart. Now it's time to show the world what I already know. You're a good person. You matter. You're loved."

He hugged her intensely for the last time and planted a kiss that would have to last forever. "Thank you for bringing me back, Gillian. Twice. I will always love you."

"And I hold in my heart a love for you that transcends both our worlds. A love that is eternal. I love you, William Ross. Alison has me beat, though." She separated from him and backed away slowly and with a heavy heart of her own.

"Gillian . . ."

"Thank you. For everything." Her tears flowed without restraint as she, too, began to fade away. Slowly, he could see through her—until he couldn't see her at all.

Gone. He watched her die. He had a hand in her death.

Just then, the apartment changed all around him. His friends—Brian, Barry, Amy, Rebecca, Dan . . . and Alison, who was all right, considering she'd been thrown as far as it takes to make an NFL first down, all reappeared as if they were in his place all the time. Only they weren't.

Ross felt his knees buckle, but he kept his footing. He was an emotional train wreck. Inconsolable. And crying his eyes out, uncaring at that moment how he would look to his friends.

Alison offered herself for a hug. Which he gratefully accepted, followed by the other five of them. They had survived. But only William knew just how much a price he paid. That would be his secret and his alone.

As it turned out, the gang didn't miss a day of work because a water main broke in the building across the street from the CityLife offices and no one could get into their jobs until the break was sealed. It would take a couple of days to repair. Fortunately, the paper came out with a double issue the prior week so they dodged a bullet there.

In the homes of Rebecca Holm, Dan McCall, Brian Vincent, Barry Greene, Amy Lloyd, Alison Kendall . . . and William Ross— all were sound asleep for a decent amount of time. Free of any nightmares, or dreams of any kind.

Chapter 32

It was 12:50PM, and there was a knock on the door. The door opened and four people walked in.

"Now this, Will, is an intervention," said McCall, who along with Vincent, Greene and Lloyd didn't even wait for him to get dressed. Thankfully, he was already reasonably dressed as they carted him down the steps and out to Vincent's car, which sped toward the Broadway Pier in the San Diego harbor area. They quickly left the car in a parking lot, taking Ross with them, briskly walking toward the Silvergate, the local ferry that crosses the famous San Diego Bay to Coronado.

"C'mon, guys, what's this all about?"

"Will, it's a beautiful day, too much so to be cooped up in an apartment," Greene finally said, breaking a silence they had since the time they spirited him out. "We didn't see you for two days last time."

"So we took a pre-emptive action to make sure you're out and about," Amy continued.

"You know what, guys? Thanks. I do appreciate it. This time, I do need the company." The line wasn't too long to get on the 50-foot long ferry, and there weren't that many passengers. Until he noticed . . .

"Rebecca . . . you OK? Are we still friends after that verbal dust up? I never did apologize."

"We both were looking for a fight. Not just you. I wasn't jealous, just angry about how the whole thing turned."

"You OK, Will?"

"Yes, Brian, I am. In the end, I knew that Gillian's goodness would prevail. Saved me from a world that I would never escape from. I just wish that she were around to see this day, to see all of you."

"It's just incredible. She was real, as human as any of us, with feelings, emotions, flaws and everything." Greene remarked. "She only was protecting someone she truly cared for and loved. I guess all of us realized that at the dinner when you showed her off."

"Any of us, if we were in her position; I mean, think about it," McCall suggested to them, "Coming into this world as an adult, with no conception of right or wrong, only guided by the one person who had a hand in creating you. If that person was in harm's way, wouldn't you do just about anything to make sure he would be all right, even if it meant putting your own welfare secondary? That's what love can do to a lot of people. It did with Gillian."

"In the end, William, she saw what being bad was doing to her, and to the one person she truly loved. Her goodness came through," Amy reminded all of them. "Your love for her saved her."

Ross nodded, but seemed distracted, as if he was—

"Looking for somebody?" Rebecca asked him.

"You could say that, 'Becca. There's a lot we need to talk about. I didn't know if she was alive or dead after Gillian did a number on her like that. I was worried about her deluxe; all I could think about was 'am I going to see her again?'"

"Is that a fact?" a surprised Rebecca suggested.

"I thought the worst. I know what it's like to have a crush on someone only to discover they're already taken. I just . . . I don't know if I'm going to get a second chance to find out more about her."

His conversation caught the ear of someone a few people in front of him in line, wearing a yellow windbreaker with a hood.

"You know the saying, 'you never get a second chance to make a first impression'? It's a bunch of crap, if you ask me."

The person turned around and took the hood off . . .

. . . revealing Alison.

She saw Ross, his face a contorted, shocked visage, tears slowly coming down from both his eyes. He impulsively hugged her like a pro wrestler clamping a headlock on an opponent. But this was far from fake.

"Thanks—I'm not sure if my ribs do likewise, but what the hey," she quipped.

He relented, only somewhat. "Last time I saw any of you, I told y'all to get some sleep." Then he turned to Alison, and there was no fear in her eyes, quite the change from when Gillian's darker half concocted that nightmare she had. "You OK?"

"Bruised ribs, nothing serious. It's always the case; people say the most honest things when they think no one's listening. I'm so glad you made it back to us. I was so scared; I didn't know if you were a goner, either, or worse."

"That makes two of us. But I do know a setup when I see one, guys." his attention now switched to his quintet of friends, trying to be deadly serious. "I do have, as your boss the option to tickle the lot of you pink, pink being the key, operative word here."

A collective pause, until Dan spills it. "OK, you caught us. Alison asked us to corral you out of the apartment and bring you down here; said she'd kick anyone's ass who ratted her out."

"She did, did she?" Ross shook his head in mock disgust. "I think I'll have to be putting this infraction into everyone's personnel files."

"Hey, it worked, didn't it?" Alison countered as the last call was announced for the 1PM ride.

"I believe that's our cue," Vincent told the others as they stepped out of line and began to walk away.

"Wait a second, aren't you guys coming?"

"Not today," Lloyd yelled. "No sweat, though. You won't be alone." She motioned to his newly acquired lunch date.

"Looks like the other shoe just dropped," Holm grinned from ear to ear. "Did we do good, Alison?"

"Oh yeah. See, Will, admittedly a unique, though roundabout way of asking you out, no?"

Ross's face was several shades of ever-changing red. But he never felt better. "I'd say it was bloody damn brilliant." He hugged Alison who gently motioned for him to go on the ferry, which he obliged. His co-workers; his lookouts, really, waved their goodbyes from the dock as the Silvergate began its one-hour sightseeing cruise to Coronado. William and Alison sprinted up to the second deck of the boat to get an even better view of the city's spectacular bay, waving back to them all the while.

Alone, finally.

"Alison, I appreciate—and marvel—at the lengths you went to get me here. I do. But as good as this feels, as right as it feels, I don't know if I'll end up being worth all of this. I hope I'm worthy of you."

"Will, there's something you need to know about last night." Alison began tentatively, measuring her words.

"What about?"

"When I kissed you while you were fending off Gillian's dark side—"

"What do you mean?" Ross was beyond confused. "I did see you, yes. That was only because Gillian morphed into you—became you. She sealed all of you out of her domain when she beat you up and kidnapped me."

"That's not entirely true." Alison kissed him one more time, as long and with as much passion as when Gillian's good and evil sides squared off. The exact same way he was kissed when trapped in his apartment. When she was done, she saw Ross's face turn ghost-white.

"As omnipotent as Gillian came off as, she couldn't duplicate to the last drop a kiss by someone she barely knew. She was good enough, however, *to bring me into the battle*, only for a moment, because she knew you were on the ropes. She knew how much I cared about you. Gillian threw you a lifeline—as it turned out, me. I haven't told a soul what I just told you, and I won't tell anyone else. They wondered where I was, and I said I didn't know because I blacked out. But I didn't."

"My God . . . it *was* you. I don't know what to say, Alison."

"You said all you needed to when you kissed me. I really, really like you, William Ross. There; I've said it out loud. No more keeping it inside me. You now know how I feel. What good is it if you keep your feelings bottled up, if you like someone, or—"

"Love someone." Ross finished her thought. They kissed once

more, but for the first time in the time he's known her off and on for the past 3 years, he initiated the kiss, and did so as if it were his last night on earth. A half-minute later, they both came up for air, the ferry purring along the bay, the top deck nearly to themselves.

"You know the best part about this one-hour ferry ride?" Alison asked.

"What's that?"

"It takes an hour to get back, too. Extra time for us to see things. To talk. To take a chance. To connect."

"Perhaps." He brought his arm around her waist and they walked toward the front of the top deck of the ferry to take in the view, talking softly.

Someone else was on the ferry, watching the events unfold in the background, unseen by them—or anyone.

Gillian.

She nodded her head—and smiled. Then she vanished, for the final time. Her last image of him was as she had hoped. Happy. At peace. Maybe, on his way to true love at last.

As the ferry went into the heart of San Diego Bay, a breathtaking cloudless sky lay before them—and peaceful waters underneath. For William Ross, after what's happened to him the past three months or so, he figured he was due.

www.ingramcontent.com/pod-product-compliance
Lightning Source LLC
Chambersburg PA
CBHW031608260626
47154CB00020B/1722